The Opportunists

The Opportunists

A Novel

Yohann de Silva

iUniverse, Inc.
New York Bloomington

The Opportunists
A Novel

iUniverse books may be ordered through booksellers or by contacting:

iUniverse
1663 Liberty Drive
Bloomington, IN 47403
www.iuniverse.com
1-800-Authors (1-800-288-4677)

ISBN: 978-1-4401-6442-2 (sc)
ISBN: 978-1-4401-6441-5 (ebook)
ISBN: 978-1-4401-6440-8 (dj)

Library of Congress Control Number: 2009937239

Printed in the United States of America

iUniverse rev. date: 9/18/2009

Dedicated to my mother, Reeta

I am who I am because of her

Kazakhstan
Shymkent
Kyrgyzstan
Tashkent
Uzbekistan
Samarqand
Tajikistan
Uzun
Turkmenistan
Termez
Mazar-e Sharif
Afghanistan

Introduction

Until the turn of this century, Uzbekistan was to Westerners a largely unknown and insignificant country. It was a small republic on the outskirts of the Soviet Union for much of the twentieth century. Even after Uzbekistan gained independence from the Soviets in 1991, the West kept the country at arm's length, writing it off as already being within Russia's sphere of influence.

September 11 changed America's perception of the world, particularly of Central Asia. Uzbekistan's potential to act as a buffer against the spread of radical Islam and its location near a major theater of military operations drew the attention of U.S. policymakers. The United States saw in Uzbekistan a valuable partner in the war on terror and a major launching point for Operation Enduring Freedom, aimed at destroying the Taliban and Al Qai'da in Afghanistan. As a result, the United States and Uzbekistan signed the Status of Forces Agreement in October 2001, guaranteeing the free use of the Karshi-Khanabad (K2) Airbase to U.S. forces. In return, Uzbekistan received more aid and economic assistance than any other Central Asian country.

Uzbekistan's poor human rights record and authoritarian rule were no longer of primary concern to U.S. policymakers, given the benefits a positive relationship would provide to the war on terror.

Many Uzbeks hoped that closer ties with the West would mark the beginning of democratization and the rule of law. Uzbekistan, however, continued to be a police state where a strong security apparatus ensured the perseverance of a repressive form of government, and wide-scale corruption crippled the economy, forcing millions of Uzbeks to survive by any means.

Part I: New Beginnings

Chapter One

Mazar-e Sharif, Summer 1978

Two young men waited in a mud-walled, one-room house on the outskirts of Mazar-e Sharif in northern Afghanistan. The late evening air was cool—a pleasant change from the midday summer heat. The inside was lit by candles and a dim oil lantern. The floor was covered with worn, faded carpets that once, a long time ago, may have held red, orange, and brown symmetrical patterns. The shorter, white man with dark brown hair sat cross-legged, while the taller, darker man squatted, his feet flat on the floor. Between them were two trays. One held a decorative tea pot and five matching cups, two of which were filled with green tea. The other held four loaves of warm naan bread. The two men had been sitting in silence, nibbling at the naan and sipping their tea for some time.

The white man was growing impatient, absently tracing a

pattern on a rug with a finger and checking his watch every few minutes. When there was a noise outside, he froze and listened attentively. He shifted often in the long robe he was wearing, uncomfortable in the Uzbek garb that was completely unnatural to him. It was meant to help him blend into the mostly Uzbek population here in northern Afghanistan, but it could not disguise the man's Russian ethnicity. He wore it nonetheless, believing it might make the difference between success and failure, life and death.

There was good reason for concealing his identity: Moscow-backed Afghan Communists had recently taken over Afghanistan in a bloody coup, killing the prime minister. The Soviet Union immediately recognized the new government and showered Afghanistan with military and economic aid. But the tribal regions in northern and eastern Afghanistan resisted the reforms the new government was imposing. These reforms included the socialist redistribution of land, granting women new marriage rights, and outlawing certain tribal customs. Tribal leaders and mullahs rebelled, and the government reacted harshly to the resistance by arresting and imprisoning many of them. People in the countryside took up arms and attacked Afghan army posts, taking control of large areas in the north and east.

Yury Popov, the Russian in Uzbek clothing, was a young captain with the Soviet Red Army's 108th Motorized Rifle Division, located in Termez, a city north of Mazar-e Sharif, just inside the Soviet Union. To say that the local inhabitants disliked him would be an understatement. And Yury had not left the relative safety of the Soviet Union to travel to northern

Afghanistan on routine official business. Tonight was one of the most important nights of his life.

"Be patient, Yury. These things take time. You've come this far. Don't do anything to sink the deal by being in a hurry," the man across from Yury said in Russian. He was Kurbon Usmanov, a Soviet Uzbek who was the key to making Yury a significant amount of money.

Kurbon also worked in Termez, providing local supplies and foodstuffs to the Red Army post. He was a citizen of the Soviet Socialist Republic of Uzbekistan. A logistical officer, Yury had naturally developed a working relationship with Kurbon. In a short time, the two had become friends, and Yury discovered that Kurbon had a brother living within the ethnic Uzbek community, across the border in Afghanistan. This fact would have threatened Kurbon's ability to do business with the Red Army, had Yury disclosed it to his superiors, but he didn't. Instead, he saw an opportunity.

Yury had had enough of the Red Army and feared his country's military involvement in Afghanistan. He had been away from his motherland in Ukraine for so long he could barely picture the countryside or the faces of his family. All indications were that he would not see Ukraine again for years. Over time, he had come to the conclusion that he needed to leave the military and the Soviet Union. He just never knew how he was going to do it. It was a dangerous undertaking and not to be taken lightly. The very thought of fleeing was enough to land him in jail, if not worse. He also needed money to escape. Otherwise he would not make it far. Kurbon's family connection to northern Afghanistan provided the solution he needed. Yury had access to thousands of Kalashnikovs stockpiled at his base for delivery to the new Moscow-friendly Afghan military. But he knew that the antigovernment insurgents in Afghanistan also needed weapons. So he decided to divert some of the stockpile to them.

It hadn't taken much to bring Kurbon into the scheme. Yury offered 40 percent of the profits to Kurbon and his brother to broker the deal. Kurbon immediately contacted his brother Mavlud, who set up the sale in a matter of weeks. A date and time were set, and Kurbon and Yury left Termez, driving into northern Afghanistan under the cover of delivering provisions to an exhausted Afghan army post in Mazar-e Sharif. If all went well, Yury would never set foot in the Soviet Union again.

The door to the small house quietly creaked open, startling the two men. A small boy with short, black hair and a round face entered, carrying another teapot with steam shooting out its snout. He was wearing a knee-length shirt and cotton pants. "That's a good boy," Kurbon said kindly, as he carefully took the pot from the child and set it down on the tray. He pulled the boy toward him by his waist and then tousled his hair. "Ravshan, your father will be back soon, okay? Now you just sit quietly and wait over there." The child scampered over to the shadowy corner and squatted against the mud wall, staring at Yury and Kurbon.

Yury didn't like the kid being around. It unsettled him. But the child was Mavlud's son and lived in the adjoining house, so he had to put up with his presence. The wooden door was still ajar, so Yury stood up to stretch his legs and walked to the door. He opened it a bit wider and looked outside. He could see in the distance the bright blue dome of the famous Blue Mosque, prominently located at the city's center. He strained to see the dark outlines of the brown, single-story buildings, similar to the one he was in, cramped together throughout the city. Yellow lights flickered through windows and doors in the otherwise dark landscape. He glanced toward the truck parked next to the house, satisfied that it—and the crates of rifles stored inside—were undisturbed.

Yury heard the sound of a jeep rumbling toward the house. He hurriedly closed the door and sat down on the worn carpet, facing the door. Kurbon noticed Yury's anxiety and said, "You should let my brother and me do the talking. We are familiar with their ways. And they will not appreciate your presence here. I'm sure you can understand why." Kurbon paused and waited for Yury to confirm that he understood, but he only received a frozen stare in response. "We'll take care of this, okay, comrade?"

Yury finally nodded, frustrated that the negotiations were going to be out of his control, but he realized that what Kurbon said made sense. The little boy, also hearing the jeep approach, stood up expectantly. Kurbon turned to the boy and said, "Ravshan, go and get some more bread for our guests." The boy hesitated and then scurried away through the door, closing it behind him.

The jeep pulled up next to the house, idled for a moment, and then the engine went quiet. Several sets of feet quietly approached the door. There was a short knock and then the door was opened from outside. An Uzbek man wearing a long, knee-length shirt, a similarly long embroidered vest, and cotton pants walked in. Though Yury had never met Mavlud before, it was clear from his resemblance to Kurbon that this was his brother. The elder Usmanov wore a thin beard, while the younger was clean-shaven.

Mavlud turned and motioned for the men to enter. Yury and Kurbon stood up simultaneously to greet their guests. Three grim-faced men entered the room. They were middle-aged, fully bearded, and also dressed traditionally. They wore soft, round-top, brown wool caps called *pakuls*, and dark, embroidered *chapans*—long coats with intricate threading. Their creased, sun-baked skin gave them a hardened appearance, an effect that was enhanced by the AK-47 slung over each man's shoulder. Two of the men carried canvas sacks. They bowed slightly with their right hands flat to their chests, greeting Yury and the two Usmanovs with "salaam alaikum."

Kurbon and Yury responded with a similar gesture and then motioned for the guests to sit. They put down their sacks and leaned their weapons against the wall behind them. The small room was crowded with six people, so Yury sat outside the circle that formed around the trays of tea and naan. The Afghans glanced uncertainly at Yury but said nothing. After everyone was seated, Mavlud smiled and began speaking, gesturing to his brother and Yury. To Yury's annoyance, Mavlud spoke in Uzbek. Yury only understood a fraction of the conversation—not enough to follow what was being discussed. Protocol dictated that Mavlud speak, since he was the elder of the two brothers, and a local.

Mavlud and the visitors did not begin by discussing the arms sale. It was customary to spend some time getting to know each other and establishing a common kinship before conducting such an important transaction. They discussed the weather, the terrain, harvests, their families, and, most important, the socialist reforms the government in Kabul was attempting to impose throughout the country. Mavlud's little son Ravshan came in and offered more bread and then squatted against the wall on the opposite side of the room, watching quietly. The three visitors understood the routine and appreciated adherence to custom, but it was apparent that they were preoccupied with Yury's presence. They scowled in his direction and occasionally whispered among themselves in the midst of the general conversation. Finally, the man who appeared to be in charge of the group spoke. "It was not clear to us that you obtained the Kalashnikovs from a Russian businessman."

Kurbon and Mavlud looked at each other. The elder Usmanov gestured toward Yury and said, "He is not a businessman. Yes, he is Russian, but his role is necessary. He is a soldier in their army, and he stole the weapons in order to sell them to you. He took a big risk coming here, but he believes in your cause."

"I'm not an idiot. He believes in the cause of making money. I was more inclined to give you a handsome price before, when I thought the money was going to fellow Uzbeks," the leader responded. Everyone sat frozen for a long moment. "I'm going to have to reevaluate my offer."

Kurbon leaned forward and said, "From where did you think the Kalashnikovs were coming? We don't produce them here. Even the ones you carry are Russian-made. You knew very well these weapons were coming from Termez."

Mavlud rested a hand on Kurbon's shoulder and pulled him back, indicating that he wanted his brother to stop speaking. The leader of the three visitors had a deadly look on his face. "I don't appreciate your brother's disrespectful tone, Mavludakka."

Mavlud chuckled uncomfortably. "Pardon my young and foolish brother. He means no disrespect. However, he is right. It went without saying that these weapons were coming to you through a Russian source. Three hundred rifles at fifty dollars each is an excellent price."

"I don't like it. I'm going to have to reduce my offer by twenty percent."

Yury felt the tension rise in the room. He needed to know what was going on. He quietly spoke to Kurbon in Russian. "What's happening?"

"These bastards are playing games with us. They are dropping their offer by twenty percent. But don't worry. We'll take care of it," the younger Usmanov whispered back.

The leader of the three stood up. "I speak Russian, you fool! Do you think we are playing games?" Kurbon appeared shocked and embarrassed by this revelation. The leader's associates also stood up, eyeing their weapons behind them.

Yury feared the conversation was spiraling out of control. And the concerned look on Mavlud's face indicated that their position was not going to improve. At best, the negotiations would end, and everyone would walk away; at worst, these men might kill them. Either way, it meant the end of Yury's chances of leaving the Red Army, and his current life, behind him. He had to make a choice.

The Russian lunged from his sitting position to one of the Kalashnikovs leaning against the wall and grabbed it. Lying on the ground, he pointed it at the three men. Rather than killing them, he hoped to scare them into leaving without their money. To his disappointment, the Afghans were not intimidated by his threat and rushed toward him to wrestle the weapon away. Mavlud managed to tackle the leader, the two of them crashing down onto the trays, shattering the tea pots and cups. Yury let out one short burst of fire into the other two men before they reached him. They fell on top of him, crushing him on the floor. They writhed in pain from the bullet wounds, but Yury pushed them aside and stood up. Then he sprayed the two with machine gun fire again until they lay motionless on the ground.

Mavlud and the leader were still wrestling frantically on the tray and the broken shards of porcelain in the center of the room, while Kurbon stood against the wall watching in horror. Ravshan stood in the corner, screaming, tears streaming down his face. Neither of the wrestling men seemed able to establish control over the other. Yury stood watching, his weapon pointed at them, but he could not get a clean shot at the Afghan leader.

Suddenly, Mavlud screamed in pain, eyes wide with surprise. He went weak and stopped fighting. The leader had plunged a knife into the elder Usmanov's stomach and was twisting it, gritting his teeth with the effort. The two men had finally stopped moving, so Yury stepped forward, rested the muzzle of the Kalashnikov against the insurgent's head, and fired one shot, killing him instantly.

Mavlud lay, twisting in pain, groaning with the struggle to stay alive. Ravshan sobbed, holding his father's face. Kurbon stood frozen, staring at his brother. He moved toward Mavlud and fell down to his knees. "I'm sorry! This is my fault," Kurbon said, choking back tears.

Mavlud spoke with difficulty. "You need to leave Mazar. It's not safe for you here. Their friends will come for you." He groaned in pain, the front of his clothing soaked in blood. He reached for his son and pulled him close. "Please, Kurbon. Take care of my son for me."

"I will. Of course I will," Kurbon said as he held his brother and stroked his hair. He continued apologizing in a soft, grief-stricken voice until Mavlud finally died. Kurbon rested his head on his brother's chest and wept. Ravshan whimpered quietly, not fully comprehending his father's death, but understanding that something terrible had just happened.

Yury stood in the corner. He felt helpless, staring at the dead men in front of him. The candles and the lantern shone an eerie yellow light onto the scene. Noticing the two canvas sacks against the wall, he knelt, opened the bags, and began digging through them. They were filled with Pakistani rupees worth thousands of dollars. This was the money he had wanted, and now he had it, at a high cost to his friend. He grabbed one of the canvas bags and slung it over his shoulder, the Kalashnikov now slung over the other. "I'm sorry about what happened, Kurbon, but I need to go." He kicked the remaining bag on the floor. "This half is yours."

Kurbon looked up at Yury, his face still wet with tears. "Fine, but I'm also keeping the three hundred Kalashnikovs we brought."

"Keep them. I only need the jeep."

Kurbon fished through his brother's pockets and found the keys. He tossed them up to Yury. "Where are you going?"

"To the Pakistani border. After that, I don't know."

Kurbon nodded. "Good luck," he said flatly, staring at his brother's body. He pulled Ravshan close to him and gently wiped the tears from the child's cheeks. "We also need to go. But don't worry, Ravshan. I'm going to take care of you."

Yury opened the door, took one last look at his friend, and left the house. The gunfire must have attracted some attention, because nearby residents had come out of their homes and peered at him from the shadows. Ignoring them, he got into the jeep and drove away, fading into the night.

* * *

Three days later, Kurbon Usmanov returned to Termez alone,

claiming to have dropped off all the weapons at the newly built Red Army base in Mazar-e Sharif. When questioned at the Soviet border about the whereabouts of the truck and the soldier assigned to the supplies, he simply said that Captain Popov had come down with a life-threatening fever and had stayed in the field hospital in Mazar-e Sharif, insisting on keeping the truck for his return journey. Kurbon rattled off his Soviet background and travel authorization in fluent Russian, and the information matched what was written on the border guard's log sheets, so he was allowed to re-enter Termez.

The period between his brother's death and his return to Soviet Uzbekistan had been difficult. After fleeing Mazar-e Sharif with Ravshan, his brother's widowed wife, and the truck full of arms, Kurbon had reached out to the remaining members of his estranged family in northern Afghanistan. A sympathetic uncle sheltered him, and he managed to liquidate the Kalashnikovs and the truck quickly for a less-than-reasonable price, spreading most of the wealth to Mavlud's wife and his Afghanistan-based relatives. He easily converted his remaining currency into rubles on the black market. Promising to stay in touch, Kurbon returned to Uzbekistan.

Kurbon did not see or hear from Captain Yury Popov again. There was an investigation, and he was questioned by military police. The truck, the weapons, and Captain Popov had all gone missing, and they believed Kurbon was complicit. He explained that Popov was the one who had ordered him to find his way back to Termez. Kurbon admitted that Yury had complained about his time in service, missed his family, and was critical of the Soviet presence in Afghanistan. But the Soviet military authorities, having nothing with which to charge Kurbon, and distracted by the impending invasion of Afghanistan, dropped the case against him.

As promised, Kurbon had remained in touch with his extended family in northern Afghanistan. They had been distant at first, but Mavlud's death had strengthened their relationship and brought everyone together. Kurbon became the sole financial supporter of Mavlud's wife and Ravshan. He was happy to provide this assistance and did so without hesitation. He felt responsible for their well-being.

His newfound connections in Afghanistan, the financial strain of taking care of Mavlud's family, and the small fortune he acquired that fateful night in Mazar-e Sharif came together to inspire an idea for how he was going to move forward with his life. He used his family network to slowly build a trafficking ring, with most of the dangerous legwork done by him alone. He smuggled all kinds of contraband into Soviet Uzbekistan. He met the needs of both poor and wealthy Russians—bringing in refrigerators, spices, clothing, and Western movies. After the Soviet Army invaded Afghanistan in late 1979, military traffic crossing the border increased, and Kurbon used this to his advantage. The large amount of money he had acquired from the sale of Yury's stolen Kalashnikovs helped him get through the border checks, acquire travel documents, and pay off soldiers to help him transport the goods.

Kurbon prospered during the war in Afghanistan. In time,

he purchased the documents necessary to bring Ravshan into Uzbekistan, where he raised him like his own son. They lived a frugal life with few indulgences and moved to Tashkent in 1987, extending Kurbon's network of traffickers to the capital. After the Soviet Union collapsed and Uzbekistan declared its independence, Kurbon began gradually affording himself small luxuries, so as to not draw too much attention to himself. His good fortune and success continued without interruption for many years.

Chapter Two

Brighton Beach, Summer 1982

Sergey Ivanov stood in his small bathroom, his face inches from the mirror, examining his cheeks and neck to make sure he had not missed any patches of hair while shaving. He stretched out portions of his leathery, creased skin and examined them again closely. Satisfied, he lathered his face with aftershave and slicked back his thinning hair with oil. He leaned back from the mirror and looked at his face again, this time staring solemnly into his own dark eyes. He stood there frozen for a moment.

He considered the many years he had lived, both in Leningrad and in New York. He thought about the challenges he had faced in emigrating to the United States, starting a new life, and becoming a small business owner. He had done it all on his own. He should have felt invigorated, but instead he felt deflated. He had left the doctor's office a few hours ago, but his mind had been clouded ever since. He had drifted home slowly and then moved about his apartment as if he were sleepwalking. "Heart disease. I can't believe it," he whispered to his image in the mirror. He shook his head slowly, as if he was disappointed in himself.

He moved out of the bathroom and threw on the weathered corduroys, button-down shirt, and cardigan laid out on his bed. He grabbed the bouquet of carnations on the kitchen counter and walked out of his second-floor apartment. The public hallways in his building were dimly lit and littered, and some corners smelled of urine. But he had moved here ten years ago, settled in, and never developed the inclination to leave. He slowly walked up two flights of stairs, thinking about how he would rather spend the evening in bed, or at least in front of the television in his apartment, alone. He reached the door of an apartment on the fourth floor and stood quietly outside it, listening to the sounds of commotion and laughter coming from inside. He forced himself to take on a more cheerful expression, and with great reluctance he knocked on the door.

A slim, blonde woman opened the door with a wide smile. She was pretty—about thirty years old, but looked much younger. "Uncle Sergey. Welcome. Please come in," she said warmly in Russian as she opened the door wider and beckoned excitedly for him to enter.

"Katya, thank you for inviting me. Please, take these flowers for your home." Sergey forced himself to smile. "You look beautiful this evening, as always. Living in the United States suits you."

Inside, the one-bedroom apartment had a pleasant, welcoming atmosphere. There was Russian classical music playing quietly in the background. Sergey's nephew, Alexander, was moving between the narrow kitchen and the small, circular dining table setting down dishes and platters of food. His and Katya's six-year-old son, Peter, was already seated at the table. He had a toy car in his hand, and he moved it across his place mat, making an engine noise with his mouth.

"Peter, put that thing away and get ready for dinner!" Katya spoke in a stern tone, but her smiling countenance didn't convince the boy. He continued to play with the car, oblivious to his mother and great-uncle.

Alexander walked out of the kitchen waving a bottle of wine in one hand. He had his father's square face and sharp eyes and flecks of gray in his jet-black hair. "Good evening, Uncle. Care for a glass of wine?"

"Alex, I would love a glass."

"Dinner is almost ready, so feel free to sit at the table." And then Alexander added sheepishly, "We aren't completely furnished yet, so there's not much else outside of the kitchen and dining room, unless you want to sit on some boxes."

"No problem. The dining table sounds great. I'm easy to please," Sergey said as he walked to Peter, rumpled the boy's dark hair, and sat down next to him. "Everything smells great, kids."

Katya walked into the kitchen to help her husband dish the cooked food onto platters and ladle the soup into individual bowls. "Well, this is the least we can do to thank you for everything you have done for us," she spoke from the kitchen. "If it wasn't for your help getting us settled, I don't know where we would be."

Sergey balked theatrically. "You're exaggerating what I've done."

"No. It's true," Alex said, delivering a bowl of cabbage soup to his uncle. "You found us this apartment and gave us jobs."

"You're both working in my little store, and thank goodness. I need the help. It's very difficult to find people I can trust, so I'm glad you two came along. There are a lot of greedy crooks out there."

Alexander next brought out a platter of *pelmeni,* a kind of dumpling filled with minced meat. He and Katya then sat down at the table. "Speaking of greedy crooks, I gave that kid Boris the envelope under the register, as you instructed." After a pause, Alex continued, "That was money in the envelope, wasn't it?"

Sergey shifted uncomfortably in his chair. "It's a necessary expense. I don't really have a choice in the matter."

"But it seemed like a lot. Can you afford it?"

"Not really, but like I said, I have to pay. Everyone pays."

"And what do you get in return?" Alex asked.

"I am able to operate the store without any problems."

"Well, that ridiculous," Katya said.

Sergey gave a weak smile. "Katya, things are very different here in New York. You have only been in the United States for a couple of months. This is not the Soviet Union, where the government runs and controls everything. Russians here have more freedom and opportunities to do what they want with themselves. Unfortunately, some of those Russians have followed criminal pursuits. And a few here in Brighton Beach, like Yury Popov, for instance, have become powerful. Unlike in Russia, bureaucrats aren't the only ones who need bribes here."

"Who is this Yury fellow?" Alex asked.

Sergey shook his head. "A defector. He came here about five years ago. He used to be in the Soviet Army, and he was in Afghanistan when the war started. He must have worked some kind of deal with the U.S. government."

"What kind of deal?" Katya asked.

"I'm guessing he told them everything he knew about the Russian forces and war plans in exchange for asylum of some kind. He had money when he got here. I'm not sure how, but he did. Yury's a private man, so these are the things I've heard from others. I'm not sure if any of it is true." He shrugged to indicate that he knew nothing else. He wanted to change the subject. "So Peter, are you excited to start school soon?"

The boy had put his car away and was quietly eating some *pelmeni*. "Yes," he said with no enthusiasm or eye contact.

"You haven't made many friends yet, but I'm sure you will once school starts. That's something to look forward to, isn't it?"

"I suppose."

Katya chuckled and lovingly rubbed Peter's small shoulders. "He's been having a difficult time adjusting. He misses his old friends in Leningrad."

Sergey nodded knowingly. "Leaving everything behind and moving to a new country is difficult, but much better for children. He'll have an easier time with English. Plus, Brighton Beach is full of Russians, all immigrants, like you, Peter. That's why everyone calls this place Little Odessa. I'm sure you'll quickly find some other boys your age to play with."

They waited for the boy to comment, but Peter sat quietly without a word, still focused on his *pelmeni.* His father finally spoke. "Hey, Uncle, didn't you say that you were going to see a doctor today about your chest pain? How did it go?"

Sergey wrinkled his face and looked away. He didn't say anything for a moment, and Katya and Alex glanced at each other in worried confusion. "Kids, the doctor told me that I have heart disease." He then forced a smile to lighten the mood. "But don't worry. This is good news for you. I need to start spending less time working at the store, which means that you will have to put in more hours and take more responsibility. And that means more pay, of course. I told you that I was glad you were around to help."

"Oh, Uncle, I'm really sorry. We will do whatever we can to help," Katya said, looking very distressed.

"But what does this mean? Do you have to take medicine?" Alexander asked.

"I have to take a whole series of medications. I'm still not sure about everything I have to do."

"But this will be very expensive. How can you pay for this, pay us more, and pay Popov at the same time?"

"I have some savings. I think that may be enough for a while."

"And after you have spent all of your savings? Then what?"

"I will have to speak to Popov and see what he can do."

Alex shook his head in disgust. They all resumed eating silently. After a moment, he said, "Again, I'm sorry to hear about your health. Please let us know if there's anything we can do for you. We are happy to help in any way that we can."

Sergey Ivanov sat on his couch in the darkness and cried violently into his hands. The only light came from a street lamp outside that shone through his living room window. He had returned to his apartment an hour ago, but he still wore his heavy coat and winter boots. He did not have the will to leave the couch, much less undress and get into bed.

He wished he could turn back the clock. It had been only three months since the dinner with his niece and nephew and their son Peter. If he could go back to that moment, he would have done things differently. He would have tried much harder to find the money. But it was too late now.

Sergey had been playing cards in his apartment with his old friend Dima, who had immigrated to the United States around the same time, in the early 1970s. They had finished a light dinner, and the card game of Durak was moving slowly because they were also busy reminiscing and watching television. The phone rang, and Sergey had only reluctantly answered it, annoyed at being disturbed. The caller was a regular customer at his convenience store, and she was frantic. She stuttered that there had been a shooting, and there were police cars outside the store. Sergey slammed down the phone, grabbed his coat, and left the apartment. Dima followed, alarmed by the look on his friend's face.

The two slogged through the snow to the store as fast as possible. Everywhere he needed to go was within walking distance of his apartment. He cared little for places that were a hassle to reach. He saw the red and blue flashing lights of the police cruisers long before his store came into view. "Nothing good can come of this," his friend muttered in Russian, breathing heavily.

Sergey reached his store, but he was not allowed in. A police officer kept a small crowd of onlookers at bay, and even after Sergey furiously declared that it was his store they were in, the officer insisted that he stay outside but remain close. Sergey looked through the glass windows of his store and saw people and movement inside but couldn't determine what was happening. "You must let me in! My family working inside! Where they? What happened?" Sergey's English deteriorated when he was emotional or tired.

"Wait here. I'll be back," the officer outside muttered and stepped into the store.

A moment later the officer walked out, followed by a grizzled man in a heavy gray coat. "You're the owner of this store?"

"Yes. What happened?"

"What is your name?"

"Sergey Ivanov."

"And you said you had family working here? Can you describe them?"

"Yes. Thin woman with blonde hair, and thin man with very black hair. Both in early thirties."

The grizzled man's face softened. "I'm sorry, Mr. Ivanov. We believe a robbery took place here." He paused for a second, and glanced uneasily at the uniformed officer next to him. "The two people you just described were killed. We think the robbery went bad, and they might have resisted. It's really difficult to say conclusively at this point."

Sergey's vision blurred and his muscles weakened. His hands reached out blindly for something to grab on to. Dima wrapped an arm around him. "Brother, I'm very sorry about this," his friend said.

The uniformed officer had quietly stepped away to keep the onlookers away, but the detective stood there silently. Tears streaked down Sergey's face. "Who did this? You catch him?"

"We don't have any leads yet, but we'll conduct an investigation. We are going to do everything we can. I promise. First, we need you to answer some questions." The investigator searched Sergey's face. "Any idea who might have done this? Do you have any enemies of any kind?"

"Enemies? I don't have enemies."

"Has anyone threatened you recently?"

Sergey's throat constricted. "No. I haven't received any threats."

The detective said nothing for a moment. "We can do the full interview tomorrow. It doesn't have to be tonight. Here's my card. Call me in the morning."

Dima took the card. "You should go home and get some rest," the detective said and then turned and walked away.

Sergey stood there in the cold and stared helplessly at his little store. His body shook slightly, and his old friend looked at him with concern in his eyes. Dima asked, "Do you think Popov did this?"

In his apartment, Sergey thought about this question. He had gone to Yury Popov's home the week before and explained his heart disease diagnosis and that he had depleted all of his savings on medication. Sergey had pleaded with Popov to let him pay less from here on out. The Ukrainian had been sympathetic but said he couldn't allow it because it would set a bad precedent. Sergey had begged him to reconsider, explaining that he would not be able to pay for medication and would die if he continued making full payments. Yury had said he would think about it and had left it at that. Now Sergey was confused. Had there been a misunderstanding?

He wiped the tears from his face and looked at the clock. It was late, and had his niece and nephew been alive, they would be arriving home by now to their son Peter. What a terrible situation, he thought dejectedly. He felt responsible for Katya and Alex's deaths, but didn't know what he could have done differently. What he was certain of was his responsibility to take care of Peter. He had no other choice. He was the only family Peter had now.

With that thought in mind, he slowly stood up. It was time to go upstairs and tell the child what happened.

Yury Popov felt alone among the crowd at Green-Wood Cemetery. He was dressed in a black suit and heavy coat, blending into the gathering of black attire, worn not by friends but by business associates, employees, household staff, and people who wanted to ingratiate themselves to him. His three-year-old daughter Anna stood next to him but was huddled against her nanny, Maria. He felt detached even from her. The morning sun shone on his face but provided little warmth. The weather was bitterly cold and he could see the misery on everyone's faces, which helped them better play the role of grieving loved ones. He decided to ignore everyone else and pretend that he and his daughter were the only ones attending his wife's funeral.

Dirt was already being shoveled over the dark casket, and those standing on the periphery of the small crowd began to peel away. He stared at the disappearing casket and considered the circumstances that had brought him here. His wife had died in childbirth. The day before, he had buried his stillborn second daughter. He thought again about the last few months of his wife's life and how poorly he had treated her. After his wife gave birth to their first daughter, Anna, Yury had wanted to try again to have a son. His wife reluctantly complied, but five months later, they discovered that she was carrying another girl. Yury blamed her and became withdrawn from both his wife and daughter. He knew that he was being irrational and unfair, but he spent less time with his family nonetheless. He was genuinely busy as well. His enterprise was growing, and he dared not become complacent, out of fear that his fragile good fortune would slip away.

But deep down, Yury knew that his busy schedule was also an excuse to avoid being at home. His household staff had urged him to spend time with his wife during the last few months of her pregnancy. He knew, from the short periods of time he was at home, that his wife was suffering from depression and was not eating well, but he assumed her sullen mood would pass with time. He was wrong. She was in poor health by the time she gave birth, and there were complications during the delivery.

Yury looked down at his daughter, taking in her grim face. Anna had been close to her mother, and the nanny, Maria, was her next-closest friend. He might as well have been a stranger. To say that he felt guilty and regretted neglecting his family was an understatement, but he decided that there was nothing to be gained by dwelling on the past. Once things settled down with work, he vowed to spend more time with Anna.

He thought about his other family, far away in Ukraine, and wondered if he would ever see them again. He still felt like a stranger in his new country, the United States. Even though he had built himself a comfortable life, he often felt as if he didn't belong. When reflecting back on the life he had had just five years ago in the Soviet Army, he could not believe how much his circumstances had changed since his last night in Mazar-e Sharif.

He often replayed the events of that night in his mind when he was alone.

Yury and his household were the last mourners remaining, and the grave was nearly filled. "Come on, Anna," Yury said softly and put his hand on his daughter's shoulder for a moment. He began walking away, his daughter alongside him, while the nanny, housekeeper, and driver followed. As he reached the large, gated entrance to the cemetery, he noticed a red-headed young man standing to the side of the path. It was Boris, one of his employees. When Yury neared Boris, the man fell into step next to him.

"Sir, last night didn't go well. I really need to talk to you," the young man whispered uneasily. Yury gave him a hard look and then gestured for everyone else to continue on to the car. He came to an abrupt stop, as did Boris.

"Sir, I went to Sergey Ivanov's store last night. He wasn't there, but his niece and nephew were. I told them that I was there to collect the monthly payment, but I only needed half the usual amount, just as you instructed. They knew the drill. They had passed me the payments before," he said, looking around him as if someone might overhear. "The woman was behind the register, and she was indignant. She told me that Sergey was sick, and he needed the money for medicine. I told her that was why he only needed to pay half from here on out, but she said that even that amount was too much. At this point, the guy, her husband, came out of the storeroom and attempted to calm her down. She did, but he agreed with her and told me that it was unfair for his uncle to pass you such a big percentage of the little profit the store made. I told them that I didn't care what their opinion was. I was there to collect. Only to scare them, I pulled out my gun and waved it at them."

Yury shook his head in disbelief. Boris quickly continued. "When the husband saw the gun, he made a grab for it. Maybe he thought I was going to shoot them. While we were each wrestling for the gun, I accidentally shot him. It was a fatal shot, and the guy dropped to the floor. The wife started screaming. At this point, I didn't think I had any other choice but to shoot her. So I did." Boris looked at his boss, pleading silently for him to understand. "I took some money from the register to make it look like a robbery and ran from the store."

The young man stopped speaking and waited nervously for a reaction. Yury was dumbfounded. He had made it for so long without having to kill anyone. The threat of violence had been enough until now to get everyone to pay. The racketeering business was currently the backbone of his enterprise, at least until some of his other businesses were up and running. But now this irresponsible kid in front of him could tie him to a double murder. He looked around. They were standing in a wide-open area with a smattering of people around the cemetery grounds. Boris had intentionally picked this place to tell him the bad news, in public. He must have been afraid to come to Yury's office and speak to him privately.

"You will leave this city. You will leave for a long time, and take the gun you used with you," Yury ordered Boris. "If you stay, it will not be good for either of us."

The redheaded young man looked down at his boots and the trampled snow, looking unhappy with the order. "Keep your mouth shut. You can come back in a year, and if all goes well, I'll take care of you," Yury said. "You screwed this up, so you must do as I say."

Boris nodded but said nothing. Satisfied that the kid understood, Yury turned and continued down the path toward the gate, leaving Boris standing alone.

Chapter Three

Summer 1995

Peter Ivanov thought he was dying. His body ached, and his head throbbed as if it had been pounded by a hammer. He would have done anything for a full glass of water. And a couple of aspirin. He promised himself that he would never drink again. Or not as much, anyway. The sounds of clanging metal and slamming cabinet doors that he had thought were part of a dream, he now realized, were actually the sounds of his uncle moving around the kitchen. He was clearly making more noise than necessary. Peter groaned and covered his head with his pillow.

Sergey opened Peter's bedroom door. "Get the hell up. It's almost noon."

"Later."

"No. Now. You have to start work in an hour."

Peter peered out from under the pillow at his uncle. The man looked old and tired. His body mass had shriveled, and he had even shrunk a couple of inches. He used a cane to move around, even in their little apartment. Peter glared at him with venom. "Get the fuck out of my room."

Sergey's eyes hardened. "You've really turned into a piece of trash, you know that? You barely managed to graduate from high school, you fight with everyone who crosses your path, and you are constantly drunk. You don't care about anything. Your parents would have been very proud."

"Thank you for reminding me for the millionth time." Peter settled back into his sheets and closed his eyes as if he had every intention of going back to sleep.

Sergey scowled, lifted his cane, and prodded his nephew with it. "You are not leaving work this evening to hang out with your good-for-nothing friends until you have cleaned up both the store and the backroom. Otherwise you can expect to find all of your belongings out on the street. I can always use more space around here."

"Don't worry, Uncle. I will be out of your hair in no time."

Sergey gave a cold, amused smile. "Ah, yes. The U.S. Army. Let's see how well your lack of respect and hatred of authority will fit with this new plan of yours." He stepped back out of the doorway and shambled down the hall. "You'll be back sooner than you think."

Peter no longer felt relaxed enough to sleep, agitated by his uncle's lack of faith in his decision to join the army and, more important, by doubt about his own ability to survive boot camp. Peter didn't consider himself a patriot. He had enlisted because he couldn't envision any other way of escaping the depressing, dead-end life he had with his uncle, working at his little store. Peter settled for his delinquent friends because they were the only ones who put up with his gloomy, jaded attitude. He drank all the time because he was bored. He blacked out when he was drunk but didn't care because he knew he never did anything memorable. His uncle was right. Peter knew he cared about nothing.

He looked at the framed picture of himself and his parents on his nightstand. They all looked so happy. It had been taken during their first week in the United States, though Peter couldn't remember the day. As a matter of fact, he remembered very little about his parents. He could only recall blurry, isolated images, as if they were part of an old dream he had once. He knew that his parents were killed at the same store he now worked in, but not by whom or why. The crime had gone unsolved. No one doubted the perpetrator was a Brighton Beach resident. Somewhere in this world—probably even in Peter's own community—the man was walking free. Peter hoped he was wrong. He hoped the person behind his parents' deaths had lived a difficult life and then suffered a vicious death. The vice-like grip criminals had on his neighborhood was another reason Peter wanted to get away. Maybe he was being overly cynical, but he saw no opportunity to make an honest living in this neighborhood. Every honest businessman came into some criminal's sights. Two more weeks.

Peter was counting the days before he was able to put his city and his uncle behind him.

Anna Popova stepped out of the kitchen of Bistro Carmille and into the dark, littered alley behind it. She lit a cigarette before tiptoeing up the alley to a side street away from the main entrance. She left the area quickly, afraid one of her father's friends or cronies would spot her and gently escort her back to her own fifteenth birthday party. She felt out of place walking around a seedy neighborhood late at night in her black knee-length dress but took comfort in the fact that her home was only five blocks away.

Anna was having a terrible evening. The birthday party her father had arranged for her had turned out to be a guise for a business meeting with his associates. Sure, they had all wished her a happy birthday and stacked presents on the table, but the guests were mostly older men who either owed her father a favor or men with whom he wanted to develop a closer relationship. Even he had spoken only a few words to her, while occasionally toasting her or throwing her a wide, artificial smile from across the smoke-filled room before turning to huddle closely with one of the men. She had had enough of it.

The cool night gave her a chill, and the eerie silence of the neighborhood didn't help her nerves. Anna quickened her pace, throwing her spent cigarette onto the street. She rounded a corner and saw two white men—boys, really—laughing loudly as they stumbled toward her. They kept teasing and shoving each other, and her instincts told her they weren't the criminal/rapist type. She studied the sidewalk as she continued to walk toward them. The two young men noticed her and grew silent, save for a few muffled giggles. Just as she was nearly past them, the dark haired, thickly built boy stepped into her path. "Hello, miss," he said with a smile playing at the corner of his lips, his breath reeking of vodka.

Anna didn't respond. She took a step to the right, to move around him, but he quickly side-stepped in front of her. "Please let me go past."

"Are you going to a party? We have no plans and would love to go to one," the dark-haired boy said. His eyes were glazed, and he swayed slightly as he stood there. His blond-haired, freckled companion was leaning drunkenly against the wall, giggling.

"I'm on my way home," Anna said sternly. She stepped to the left, but he again moved in front of her. Suddenly angry, she gave him a hard shove, and he stumbled backward, arms flailing, before falling on his behind onto the sidewalk. He was stunned and looked at his friend as if he had no idea what had just happened to him. Anna didn't take the opportunity to run but stood frozen, amazed by her own behavior.

The young man slowly got back onto his feet, but his face was no longer jovial.

The blond-haired boy took a step toward his friend and put a hand on his chest. "Careful, Peter," he said. "This is Yury Popov's daughter."

This warning didn't put Peter on alert but rather seemed to

enrage him. He brushed away his friend's arm and quickly moved toward Anna, wrapping a hand around her neck. He slammed her against the wall. Anna, choking, fought to tear his hand away from her throat, but Peter was much stronger. "Your father is the scum of this earth, walking around like he owns this city. As if he owns all of us," he hissed at her. "And I see you are just like him." His hand gripped her throat harder. Anna was in real pain now, and tears welled up in her eyes.

The blond grabbed Peter's arm and struggled to pull him away. "Peter! Peter Alexandrovich! What the hell are you doing? You are going to get us killed!"

Peter slowly eased his grip on Anna's throat and removed his hand, but he continued to gaze into her eyes. She coughed and struggled to maintain her balance. "You are going to pay for this, you bastard," she spat out.

Peter's hand flew through the air and slapped her hard across the face. She stepped back in shock, eyes wide with terror. Her ears were ringing. She gingerly touched her fingers against her stinging cheek. She couldn't believe what was happening and wondered whether she would be able to escape. She looked into Peter's red face, and watched as the rage on it slowly faded into sadness. His shoulders slumped. "I'm not a bastard," he muttered softly and then turned and began walking in the direction from which Anna had come.

The other young man stood there, looking bewildered, his head swiveling back and forth from Anna to Peter, who was retreating down the sidewalk. He then rushed to catch up with

Peter, and the two continued walking away, leaving Anna alone again in the dark. She turned and started to run, tears streaking down her face. As the reality of what had just happened finally sunk in, she began sobbing. As much as she wanted to, she could not tell her father what had just happened. He would blame her for the incident. He would berate her for leaving the party and would punish her by not allowing her to go out at all. Her father was negligent but also overprotective. No, she couldn't tell him.

She took off her dress shoes and continued to run barefoot. "Peter Alexandrovich, Peter Alexandrovich, Peter Alexandrovich," she repeated over and over again. She didn't want to forget his name. His image was seared into her brain. She knew that she would never forget him, and she promised herself that she would have her revenge one day.

Chapter Four

Tashkent, Spring 2000

Kurbon Usmanov woke up in the late morning to plush pillows and a soft down comforter. He opened his eyes to see the humming ceiling fan above him. The bright sunlight was streaming through his window, the swaying branches of the tall tree beside it casting a moving shadow on him and his large bed. He lazily reached his limbs toward the four corners of his bed to stretch his sore muscles. He tried to recall the dream he had been having but could only remember a few images, as if it was an old memory. After lying in bed for another minute, he threw off the covers and set his feet into the cotton slippers at his bedside. He walked across the hardwood floor to the dresser and looked in the mirror above it. He glanced at the small black-and-white framed photograph of himself and his brother that stood on the dresser, comparing the images of himself, then and now. He had aged considerably over the past twenty-two years. He had gained weight all around, especially in the midsection. His face had softened and widened, his hair had thinned, and there were streaks of white by his temples. He had looked better during his younger days. He smiled lightly, not caring. He was a richer man now.

He took his time moving around his large house in Tashkent. On the patio, he read the previous day's newspaper, showered in his oversized bathroom, got dressed in a closet the size of a small bedroom, and then nibbled on the bread and jam set out by his housekeeper. His attire was simple: he wore gray dress pants with a white dress shirt, neither of which would make him stand out in a crowd. His chauffeur drove him to his office in a black 1995 BMW. He had acquired the car through a friend—used, but it was a status symbol in a country that had very few Western vehicles.

Kurbon's second-story office was located in a stretch of crumbling, gray Soviet buildings occupied by electronic shops, a butcher, two cafés, and a number of apartments. Throngs of people were on the street. Uniformed schoolgirls in black skirts and white blouses gathered in the shade, enjoying the spring weather and street-side *somsas,* which were potato-filled baked bread patties. A babushka in layers of colorful clothing was sitting on the sidewalk hawking dried river fish laid out on canvas to passersby. Kurbon walked up the flight of stairs to a nondescript door and knocked twice, then once, then three times. A moment later, the door cracked open and a half-visible face peered at him before the door opened wide.

Kurbon walked inside, pausing for a moment to observe the operation he had slowly put together over the last two decades. Against one wall stood crates of Chinese-made consumer goods, against another, stacks of rolled-up Afghan carpets. Sheets of paper of all sizes and colors pinned to a cork bulletin board took up the third wall. Along the fourth side of the room, farthest from the door, was a desk cluttered with paper, ledger books, and disassembled electronics. His nephew Ravshan sat behind the desk, managing the cyclone of people and goods moving through the office. He had soft, delicate features, and his hair was brushed forward, flat on his forehead. His stocky, square frame was dressed in a sharp black suit and a crisp, light-blue button-down shirt. Kurbon thought his nephew's attire was inappropriate for a clandestine smuggling operation and had asked him many times to dress more like the blue-collar tenants in the building. He had brought his nephew on board as an apprentice of sorts, but it was clear to Kurbon that Ravshan was enjoying his generous salary more than the work.

There were a few other people in the room stacking boxes in a corner, looking at the bulletin board, or speaking with his nephew. The man speaking with Ravshan looked confused, while his nephew appeared frustrated, pointing with exasperation at a sheet of paper before him.

"What's the problem?" asked Kurbon as he approached the desk.

"Nothing. I need to make some adjustments because some of our merchants, like Yusif here, give me incomplete accountings. I have to go back and redo all the books," Ravshan said in disgust, pointing to the man in front of him and the papers on his desk. "Plus, this week's balance sheets don't match our current inventories, either."

There was always something, the senior Usmanov thought as he looked at his nephew. Ravshan had always shown minimal interest in the work, spending very little time ensuring accuracy, speaking with the merchants, or trying to understand the products they were trading. When problems arose, he typically blamed them on others, accepting none of the responsibility. Kurbon had put his nephew through accounting courses, but they didn't seem to help.

"And remember Otobek Bobidov, from Chorsu Bazaar?" Ravshan continued. "He's been short on his payments the last three months. I called him *and* went to see him, but I can't seem to get through to him. I'm tired of putting up with his shit!"

Kurbon was skeptical. He knew Bobidov. The man had been on the books for a long time, and he never had problems with him in the past. He was positive that the error, as usual, was with his nephew. Kurbon fought the urge to slap the young man across the head. "I'll go speak with Otobek. You stay here and straighten this mess out."

The older Usmanov looked around the office one more time before turning and walking out of the office. He knew exactly why he didn't discipline his nephew more. He had always felt guilty about his brother's death, believing that Mavlud would still be alive had Kurbon not pulled him into that deal in Mazar-e

Sharif. Whenever he considered disciplining his nephew, he remembered little Ravshan's face as he witnessed his father's murder. The memory helped Kurbon keep his anger in check when dealing with the boy's idiocy. Luckily, despite his nephew, his business still moved along without any major mishaps.

Kurbon stepped into the waiting BMW and directed the driver to Chorsu Bazaar. While moving through the city, he reconsidered the decision to allow Ravshan to manage the day-to-day operations of his business. There was good reason why he needed him: the kid was loyal and would never betray him. Their fates were intertwined. Kurbon was always able to count on family when others had abandoned him. He only wished his nephew was more competent and driven, and he feared that one day Ravshan would make an error that would cost him his business. He realized that it might be time to bring in someone else to help with the office work, but he could not hand over this critical aspect of his business to just anyone.

Kurbon got out at the main entrance to the bazaar. Chorsu was one of the oldest and biggest bazaars in Tashkent. Every necessity was available here to the average Uzbek. Chorsu was also known for having the best prices—much better than those in the ethnic Russian bazaars or the smaller bazaars in more affluent neighborhoods. Price was critical, given the meager salaries average Uzbeks lived on, and thousands of Uzbeks visited this bazaar on a daily basis to buy what they needed. There was little room to maneuver: merchants and hawkers set up their stalls in every available space. As Kurbon made his way through the cramped stalls, he couldn't help but notice the steady hum of trade and the smell of grilled meats and baked breads in the air. Sellers called out to him, but he avoided eye contact with them. Meeting their eyes would only encourage them to continue pressing their wares. Officers of the militia wearing forest-green uniforms were scattered throughout the bazaar, standing in shaded areas, lazily monitoring the crowds. The Uzbek police were some of the least-educated public servants in the government, but they had enough authority to make life very difficult for the average Uzbek.

The bazaar was divided into areas for food, clothing, appliances, household items, electronics, and carpets. Kurbon headed toward the latter. Most of the merchants here offered machine-made, low-quality carpets that poorer Uzbeks used to cover the floors in their homes. A few shops, however, also operated on the black market, selling handmade rugs and carpets produced in Turkmenistan, Afghanistan, and the Uighur regions of China. These could be purchased legitimately in the open market but were expensive due to import taxes. Kurbon's rugs were smuggled into Uzbekistan to avoid the customs fees, making his rugs cheaper than his competitors'.

Kurbon entered Otobek Bobidov's shop and observed the short, hunched man in shabby, stained clothes haggling with one customer while another young couple perused the selection of machine-made rugs on display. Catching sight of Kurbon, Bobidov beckoned a young assistant behind the counter to come and help his customers. He then walked toward his guest with a toothless smile. "Ah, Kurbonjon! What a wonderful surprise.

Welcome to my humble shop." He vigorously shook Usmanov's hand and led him to the back of the store through a curtained doorway. Bobidov was well-known in Chorsu and had always managed to move his goods on a regular basis, resulting in a steady revenue flow. Few people were as established as Otobek in this business.

"Mr. Bobidov, it's a pleasure to see you. I haven't been to your shop in a long time. How is business?"

"Contrary to what you might have heard, business is fine," Otobek said as he walked to a flimsy wooden bookshelf and pushed it from one side. The bookcase scraped along the wall and floor, revealing a small metal door with a padlock. He fished through his pockets, pulled out a key, and unlocked the door. It groaned on its rusty hinges as the shriveled man pushed it open. They stepped into a small, bare, windowless room stacked with carpets. Once inside, the shopkeeper turned abruptly to face Kurbon. "If you don't mind me being frank, your damn nephew has screwed up his accountings! He told me that I received twenty Afghan and ten Turkmen carpets this last winter. Bullshit! I only received ten of each."

He started rifling through a stack of papers on a low shelf. Giving up after a minute, he poked his head out of the room and yelled, "Alisher! Come here!" "I'll prove it to you," he said in a low voice.

Otobek's young assistant hurried to the back of the store and stepped into the hidden room. He was slim, about 5'9" in height, and appeared to be in his early thirties. He had sharp Persian features, with short, straight, dark hair and a tanned complexion, like most Uzbeks. His cheeks were slightly pockmarked, probably from bad acne during his youth. He had a notebook in his hands. He nodded a greeting to Kurbon, turned to his boss, and asked, "Is this about the inventory?"

"Yes. Are those your records? Show them to Mr. Usmanov."

Alisher flipped through the notebook before turning it toward Kurbon. "These pages contain all the deliveries we have received from your office over the last six months. The pages show the carpets we have sold, the price we sold them at, and the percentage of the profits we forwarded to your office. These final few pages detail our current inventory here in this room."

Otobek nodded, a smile on his face. "As you will see, Mr. Usmanov, our records are accurate, as they have always been during our long relationship."

Kurbon was impressed with Alisher's professional bookkeeping. The pages of math were clear and understandable. There was no question that Otobek's assistant had spent a lot of time and effort on this task.

The hunched shopkeeper pointed to the notebook in Kurbon's hand. "You can take that book with you if you promise to return it. Alisher keeps a second copy, somewhere in this back room."

"That would be great. Thank you. I'll return it to you in a few days." Kurbon started to leave, slightly embarrassed by having made this visit. He stopped and turned toward Alisher. "Son, where did you learn to do your bookkeeping?"

"On my own, sir."

"Hmm. Good for you. What is your last name?"

"Akhmetov, sir."

Kurbon turned to Otobek, "Do you trust this kid with your business?"

"Of course," Bobidov scowled. "But he's mine. Find your own lackey to fix your problems."

Three days later, Alisher knocked on the door to the Usmanovs' office. The door opened and a smiling Kurbon Usmanov greeted him. "Come in, Alisher. Welcome to my office. I'm surprised you've never been here before."

Alisher stepped into the cluttered office and looked around. He saw Ravshan sitting at the desk. Alisher smiled, walked over to the desk, and extended his hand. "It's good to meet you. I'm Alisher."

Ravshan got up from his chair and shook Alisher's hand. "It's very good to meet you, Alisher. I'm Ravshan Usmanov, Mr. Usmanov's nephew. I manage this office." Ravshan let these facts sink in. "I've heard a lot of good things about you."

"Well, Mr. Usmanov is very kind to offer me a position in his office. His salary is also very generous."

Kurbon walked over to the desk and chuckled. "I also had to compensate your former boss for removing you from his hands. But don't worry. I don't expect you to know how to do everything immediately. I want you to spend the next few weeks learning the office's operations. After a month, I want you to take over the accounting for our business. You will work for, and report to, Ravshan."

"Of course," Alisher said, nodding his head toward the younger Usmanov in acknowledgment.

"You can start by inventorying the products we currently have in stock. I also rent out the adjacent unit for storage, so make sure you go through both places."

"No problem, Mr. Usmanov."

"I'll be off, then. I leave you in my nephew's hands."

Kurbon walked out of the office and into the hallway outside. His nephew chased after him. "Can I have a moment with you, Uncle?" Ravshan asked, closing the office door behind him. "I'm sure Alisher will be a good addition to our staff, but I really don't need any help in the office. Are you sure you can't find some use for him elsewhere?"

"I'm fully staffed everywhere else. Plus, I think you can use some assistance. You seem overloaded with responsibilities. Alisher will help you better manage the business by focusing on the accounting. This will free you up to manage the staff and move our products into and out of these offices."

The younger Usmanov's shoulders slumped. "If you say so."

"I do say so," Kurbon said as he began walking away. "Good luck. I'll check in later."

Ravshan watched his uncle walk down the flight of steps before returning to the office.

* * *

Alisher exceeded all expectations over the following months. Through the spring, summer, and fall, he worked diligently at every task assigned to him. During inventory, he discovered items that were previously written off as lost or destroyed. After carefully studying past accounting records, he was able to identify a worker who had "lost" products on occasion during the previous year. He also streamlined the distribution of supplies so that products never arrived at the Usmanov offices at all. Instead, the smuggled goods went straight from the traffickers to the merchants at the bazaars and shops throughout Tashkent. There was no longer any merchandise in the office to incriminate the Usmanovs in the event of a raid. No longer needing the extra space, Alisher terminated the lease for the adjoining office previously used for storage. He also suggested hiring a number of men to visit each merchant and ensure that profits were paid on time. Up to now, Kurbon and Ravshan had been personally making these visits. Kurbon agreed, since expenses had been significantly reduced. Alisher hired a few trusted childhood friends for the job.

Alisher was successful even on a personal level. In no time, he knew every trafficker and merchant by first and last name. He shared their meals, visited their families, and listened to their concerns and complaints. Everyone took a liking to him. As a result, they would often go to Alisher with problems that were Ravshan's responsibility.

Although Alisher kept him informed of such things, Ravshan increasingly felt that Alisher was encroaching on his responsibilities. Ravshan watched Alisher with resentment as he slowly became a crucial part of the Usmanov business. Ravshan abused him, giving him the most time-consuming and grueling tasks, but Alisher never complained. He excelled at everything he did and always treated both members of the Usmanov family with respect. Kurbon seemed infatuated with his prodigy and treated him like a son, rewarding him with an increasingly higher salary and greater responsibilities. This poisoned Ravshan's mind, and he began to withdraw into himself as winter approached.

Chapter Five

Winter 2000

Ravshan sat in the passenger seat of a black sedan parked in the corner of a large parking lot facing the entrance to the Sum department store, the only department store in Tashkent. A recent snowfall blanketed the parking lot. The light from the street lamps reflected off the snow, brightening the late evening. The car wasn't running, and he was freezing.

"This is a very patriotic thing you are doing," said Salim Guliyamov, the man in the driver's seat. He was an officer of the National Security Service, the country's intelligence and security apparatus, with wide-ranging authority to do whatever it took to maintain order and stability in Uzbekistan. Guliyamov blew into his hands and rubbed them together vigorously to warm them.

Ravshan was lost in thought while he looked out the windshield at the last few shoppers trickling out of the department store as it prepared to close. He felt small and was ashamed of what he was doing. But he believed that his good standing with his uncle was slipping away and that he must take action. "One of my employees is ruining my uncle's reputation and harming our business. I just want to make sure that we are working on the right side of the law."

Ravshan had called Salim and requested the meeting. Salim pulled out a pack of cigarettes from his coat pocket, withdrew a cigarette with his lips, and lit it with an old metal lighter. He slowly exhaled and filled the interior with smoke, thinking about how much he hated winter. Salim looked skeptically at his passenger and asked, "Why don't you tell me your story again?" But it wasn't a question, it was an order.

Ravshan sighed and looked at the NSS officer. Salim had a dark birthmark on his left temple and black-and-white peppered hair. His skin appeared parched from dehydration. He might once have been a fit man, but he was starting to show signs of excess. "His name is Alisher Akhmetov, and he joined my uncle's business last spring. Prior to Akhmetov's arrival, my uncle and I imported rugs, Chinese electronics, and other consumer goods. After Alisher took over the accounting, he became responsible for paying the customs and taxes on our products. But he has been living lavishly since he joined our business, and I suspect that he is pocketing the percentage that should be going to the government. I want to tell you this before we are investigated for tax evasion."

Salim smoked quietly, considering what he had just heard. He was very good at assessing people. He could look at someone and tell immediately whether the person was trustworthy, intelligent, stupid, or lying. He was not convinced this whistleblower was giving him the full story. Ravshan came across as an opportunist with a hidden agenda. Even so, Salim thought Akhmetov was worth following up on. Illegal trafficking was his portfolio, not tax evasion, but busting Alisher might be an easy way to earn some points with his service for going above and beyond his duties.

Salim cracked open the window and flicked out his spent cigarette. It hissed as it struck the snow. "Does your uncle know you're speaking with me?"

A look of horror came across Ravshan's face. "No, not at all. Do not associate me with this. Pretend that you became aware of it by scrutinizing our tax records."

Salim hated being told how to do his job. He looked at Ravshan and forced a smile. "Don't worry. I'll take it from here."

Three weeks later, Alisher stepped out of a taxi at the intersection of Shota Rustavelli and Glinka Roads and walked into a one-story structure attached to a much larger office building. The inside was completely gutted and littered with carpentry equipment. Half a dozen workers were renovating the place. Kurbon and Ravshan stood at the center of the empty room giving directions. Alisher took off his heavy coat and threw it on a stack of boxes before approaching the two men.

Kurbon turned to Alisher and smiled. "This is going to be my new restaurant. It's not much now, but in a couple of months this place should be ready to open. I'm going to call it the Café Three Oranges. It'll be a café by day and a restaurant and bar by night."

"The place looks like it has a lot of potential. I'm sure it will be a big hit."

"I appreciate your enthusiasm. I hope you're right." The older Usmanov looked around his establishment for a moment and asked, "So, to what do I owe this visit?"

Alisher paused, seeming to consider his words carefully. "Our man from the bank called this morning. He told me that someone came by today to ask about your business account. He showed his NSS credentials before asking to see your tax records for the last two years."

Ravshan, who had been standing quietly, said, "It could be routine."

Kurbon was worried. He knew that nothing good could come out of this development. He wondered what had prompted this inquiry and what he could do to safeguard his business, and perhaps his life. "What was the result of this visit?"

Alisher shrugged. "The NSS officer looked through the records, took some notes, and left without saying anything. I told our man to keep me updated if he returns."

Ravshan stood quietly, observing the carpenters' work. Kurbon pursed his lips and nodded. "Okay. Good work. Keep me updated."

* * *

Alisher Akhmetov was tired. It was late at night, but he was still in the office looking over his accountings. The previous day he had balanced the numbers on the incoming merchandise to include the commissions paid to all the traffickers. He had given these books to Kurbon for review and expected to receive nothing but positive remarks. This evening he was calculating the month's revenue based on the invoices he had received from each of the merchants. All the numbers were in order and matched the profits he expected. His records of the items the merchants had not sold matched the invoices they had provided.

Alisher was happy with his work. He considered himself to be a lucky man. He was better off, compared with his previous circumstances, when he was slaving away for Otobek. Kurbon appreciated his hard work and had rewarded him well for it. Ravshan, on the other hand, had always been cold toward him, saying nothing when he had done well and admonishing him severely for forgetting to complete tasks that were not even his responsibility. Alisher took this criticism in stride. He'd thought Ravshan's coldness would pass once he realized that Alisher contributed to the Usmanovs' success, but it never did. Alisher struggled to find a solution. He even considered bringing up the issue with Kurbon, but he knew that this conversation would not bring results that were in his favor.

While sitting at the table that Ravshan once occupied, he had begun putting away his work for the night when he heard a heavy knock on the door. Alisher froze. It was almost midnight.

He never had visitors this late. All of the traffickers, merchants, and general muscle knew better than to come by outside normal business hours. The windows even had thick black curtains to prevent the light from being seen from the street.

There was another series of heavy knocks. "Who's there?" Alisher called from behind his desk. No response. He squinted at the door as if to see through it.

Suddenly the door burst open, sending small wooden shards across the floor. Ten militia officers rushed into the room with pistols drawn. They surrounded Alisher and yelled at him to lie flat on the floor. Slowly, with his hands in the air, he dropped to his knees and lay prone.

A man in dark, Western clothing walked into the office smoking a cigarette. He looked like a zombie, with his pale, gaunt face and salt-and-pepper hair. "Alisher Akhmetov?"

Alisher stuttered a confirmation. The militia officers handcuffed him before lifting him up and sitting him back in his office chair.

Salim walked up to Alisher and stood a foot away. "We have evidence that you have not been paying your taxes and are involved in illegal trafficking. What do you have to say to this?"

"You're wrong. You're making a mistake." Alisher summoned some courage, but he knew that he was the one who had made the mistake. There was a secret compartment beneath the floorboards of the office where he placed all his papers at the end of each night. He should have put his books and invoices away the moment he heard the knocking. But he hadn't.

"So are you telling me that I would be wasting my time going through all this paperwork?"

Alisher didn't respond. He stared down at the wet footprints and melting ice the militia had tracked in.

"You're much better off confessing to everything now. Your punishment will be harsher if I have to go through a long investigation to convict you."

Alisher continued to stare at the floor. Fear gripped his throat. "I don't know what you are talking about."

Salim squatted so that he could look up at the sitting Alisher. "You're being foolish. I just need you to tell me what you're doing here in this office with all of these ledgers. I know that you're working with the Usmanovs. You are here just doing their work. Their bidding. You need to make a living, so you are only doing what you are told to do. Isn't that right?"

"I don't know what you are talking about."

A few of the militia officers chuckled.

Salim admired Alisher's courage. After going through the Usmanov bank records, Salim figured that Kurbon had been fudging his accountings for many years. Sure, he had paid taxes, but only for the small amount of profit he had claimed. Having monitored the foot traffic going in and out of this office over the last three weeks, Salim knew that the Usmanov business was far bigger than the records reflected. Usmanov appeared to be a major trafficker of contraband in Uzbekistan. Alisher was just the front man for the operation and for some reason Ravshan wanted him to take the fall. "I'm going to give you one last chance, Alisher. Just tell me you're doing all of this for Kurbon and Ravshan Usmanov. I know that this is not your own business. I can save you."

Alisher willed himself to stop trembling. He held his courage, believing that the Usmanovs would get him out of this mess. "I have nothing to say."

The ringing of his cell phone woke Kurbon Usmanov early the next morning. Irritated, he got up and walked to the dresser to see who had disturbed his sleep. It was his nephew calling, so he sighed and answered the phone.

"Uncle, you need to come into the office immediately." Ravshan's voice was shaking.

This isn't good, Kurbon thought. His nephew was not one to overreact. "Okay, I'll be there soon," he responded, not wanting to discuss details over the phone.

An hour later, Kurbon strode into his office. Ravshan was there, his face ashen. "When I arrived this morning there was no sign of Alisher, but this note was on the desk." Ravshan handed his uncle a letter written in Russian.

The older Usmanov took the letter and carefully read it:

Dear comrades,

Alisher Akhmetov has been arrested for failing to pay the taxes on imported merchandise as required by law. The records present on his desk are hereby confiscated and will be used as evidence during his trial.

If you wish to speak on Mr. Akhmetov's behalf or provide any evidence in his defense, please contact the prosecutor general's office.

If you believe that Mr. Akhmetov has been arrested in error, please contact me to discuss this issue.

Salim Guliyamov

The National Security Service

Kurbon crumpled the letter and threw it at the wall, growling out loud. The letter was in effect a request for a bribe. If Kurbon paid, the criminal case against Alisher would go away. If not, prosecution would continue. He wondered how much Alisher would divulge about the business. His entire life's work was at risk.

His nephew peered into a small cavity in the floorboards. "The ledgers on the merchant's profits are gone. None of their invoices are here, either. What are we going to do?"

The morning was particularly cold, but sweat was beading on Kurbon's forehead and neck. "I'll see how much money this man wants. I need you to get in touch with Alisher somehow. Tell him that we are going to do what we can to help him, but we need him to be silent about his work for us." Ravshan nodded, so Kurbon continued, "In the meantime, we are going to deny everything. As far as we are concerned, Alisher was acting on his own behalf."

The next day, Kurbon contacted Salim, who told him that the Usmanovs would need to pay one hundred thousand U.S. dollars for Alisher's release and to end the investigation. This was a very high figure by anyone's estimation, but in Uzbekistan it was astronomical. Kurbon did not think a hundred thousand was a reasonable amount, so he offered fifty thousand dollars instead.

Salim took the money, but he also compromised on his offer. Alisher was not released as promised. In addition, over the next several days, all the merchants identified in the ledgers were summarily arrested and all their products confiscated. The fifty thousand dollars bought the Usmanovs their own freedom, because the investigation did end as promised. But the arrest of the merchants meant that the Usmanovs' business collapsed.

Kurbon became an angry, hard man. He vowed to punish Salim Guliyamov for destroying him. He even avoided his nephew. He had no evidence, but he believed Ravshan's incompetence had led to the investigation. He isolated himself in his home, promising himself that he would somehow regain everything he had lost.

Part II: Few Options

Chapter Six

Brighton Beach, Early Spring, 2002

Peter Ivanov stared intently at the playing cards on the green felt blackjack table. He was sitting in the underground gambling hall of the Soviet and was no longer playing to win, but rather hoping to break even. The dealer was showing a six of clubs, while Peter had a queen of hearts and a five of diamonds face up in front of him. He had five hundred dollars at stake, and if he lost, he would not make his rent for the month. He had already lost seven thousand dollars this evening. The strong smell of cheap cologne wafting from the greasy-haired Estonian to his right was making his nose burn. The dealer and the other four players around the table were impatiently waiting for him to make his decision. Two of the players gave him contradictory advice on whether he should hit or stay. He took a deep drag from his cigarette and thought some more. Hit or stay, hit or stay.

He felt eyes on him from around the smoky, dimly lit gambling hall. He was a regular here, and the pit bosses knew that he was on a month-long losing streak. The seven thousand dollars he had so far lost this evening was a loan from the owner, and it was just the latest installment of the fifty thousand dollars he had slowly borrowed, and lost, during the last two weeks. Every day he'd come to the Soviet, a seedy, mob-owned bar and gambling hall in the heart of Brighton Beach. He desperately wanted to win this hand. If he did, it would allow him to hang on and potentially recoup his losses for the evening. He considered carefully. Hit or stay, hit or stay.

His hand glided onto the felt and tapped it. The dealer slid a card out of the shoe and flipped it over onto Peter's hand. It was a seven of diamonds. Twenty-two.

"Sorry, brother." The dealer took Peter's stack of chips in a sweeping motion. The dealer then pulled a card out of the shoe and dealt it to himself. The king of spades. Sixteen. He dealt himself another card. The eight of clubs. Twenty-four. The remaining five players cheered as the dealer passed out their winnings.

Peter felt like he had been slapped in the face.

The overdressed Estonian to his right nudged him with his elbow. "Better luck next time," he said in Russian. He chuckled as he counted his winnings.

Peter gave him a look that wiped the smile off the man's face. Peter stood at six feet and had a muscular frame and a crooked nose that had never set properly after being broken a long time ago. The Estonian got up and walked away.

Peter finished smoking his cigarette in silence. He couldn't wrap his mind around what had happened to his luck. While in the army, he had gambled well and won often. He returned home from his tour in the Balkans and finished his enlistment with twenty thousand in savings, most of it from winnings. Exactly one month ago, he still had that twenty grand. He had lost all of it in two weeks. Desperate, he had borrowed from the owner of the Soviet, hoping to win back his losses. Now he found himself fifty thousand dollars in debt to the kind of person to whom he never wanted to owe money. His fortunes had changed dramatically, and he saw no way out of the bind he was in.

Feeling unwelcome at the blackjack table, he pushed his chair back and stood up. He wanted to disappear without anyone noticing. He walked toward the exit, but as he reached the door, a very large man with a grim face put a hand on his chest to stop him. "Not so fast, Ivanov," he said in English but with a thick Russian accent. He casually pointed toward the kitchen doors. "The boss wants to see you in the back."

Peter's heart skipped a beat, knowing that nothing good could come out of a conversation with the Ukrainian owner. He didn't have any doubts about what the chat would be about. He put on his most confident, no-worries expression, strode to the kitchen entrance, and pushed through the double doors.

Yury Popov, the short, dark-haired owner of the Soviet, was leaning against a polished aluminum cooking table, facing him with his arms crossed. Standing around him in a half-circle were a handful of Yury's men—large, doped-up Slavic men who lacked the English-language skills, sophistication, or brainpower to assimilate into American society. They looked at him with cold, merciless faces. Two members of the kitchen staff stopped what they were doing, wiped their hands on towels, and walked past Peter into the gambling hall, avoiding eye contact with him as if he were radioactive. He was all alone now with Yury and his thugs. Peter despised the man, but his strong feelings about the presence of his kind in Brighton Beach had settled to a low simmer during his time in the military.

Yury was wearing a tacky purple double-breasted suit. Even though he was in his early fifties, he looked older because of the creases in his skin and the gray hair at his temples. He said in heavily accented English, "Tough night, Peter?"

Peter smiled. "Yury, don't worry about my loss today. I'll have the money back in your hands in a few weeks."

"And with what money do you plan on winning my fifty grand back?"

"I'll scrape some together. I'm getting paid in a few days, plus a few friends of mine owe me money."

"You don't have any friends, and the few hundred dollars you make in construction isn't going to be enough to pay back the fortune you have so skillfully managed to lose over the last month." Yury's men shifted toward Peter and began circling behind him.

"My luck is going to change, Mr. Popov. Just give me some more time," Peter said reassuringly. Glancing around him, he realized that he wasn't being convincing enough.

Suddenly, one man bear-hugged Peter across the chest from behind and another jabbed him hard in his stomach. The blow dropped him to the floor and he doubled in pain. Peter knew how to fight, and on an average day could have bested any one of Yury's thugs, but he didn't stand a chance against four of them. And fighting back wasn't going to make his debt go away. So he gasped on the floor like a wounded beast, making no effort to take on the thugs around him.

Yury took a step toward Peter. "I could kill you right now, you know? Believe me, no one is going to miss you around here. Rumor has it that you're not very good company," he chuckled as he looked down at Peter the way an owner might look down at a misbehaving dog. "I'm going to give you one very good option for getting rid of this debt. I suggest you take it. You work for me for one full year, doing everything I ask you to do, and the debt will be forgiven."

Peter pushed himself off the red-tiled floor with one arm and looked up at Yury. "No thanks, I already have a job." A hard blow to the back of the head slammed his face against the greasy kitchen floor. He felt blood dripping from his nose and his vision began to blur.

"Don't be an idiot, Ivanov. Your only other option is dying, slowly and painfully." Yury took a step back and leaned against the kitchen table.

Peter pushed himself up onto his elbows and looked again at the Ukrainian. A motion behind Yury caught Peter's attention. A slender young woman observed him from an unlit part of the kitchen. He didn't recognize her, but thought the woman's cold eyes diminished her otherwise attractive appearance. "I'll think about it," he mumbled, wanting to spare himself the physical pain of continuing the conversation. His vision came in and out of focus. Yury's men came around to either side of him, lifted him, and carried him through the kitchen doors and through the gambling hall. The men around the tables fell silent as they watched a bloody-faced Peter being taken outside. This was no doubt meant to be an example to the other patrons who had a debt with Yury Popov. Peter hung his head and let himself be carried out of the hall and up two flights of stairs and thrown out the front door onto the filthy sidewalk. Lying on his back, he ignored the pedestrians who looked down at him as they scurried past. He stared at the hammer and sickle glowing in red neon over the Soviet's entrance, wondering how he had reached such a point in his life.

* * *

After enlisting in the U.S. Army in 1995, Peter finished boot camp at Fort Benning, Georgia, and became an infantryman. He was sent to the Balkans as a peacekeeper with the Third Infantry Regiment in November 1996 as part of Operation Joint Endeavor. Its purpose was to implement the military elements of the Dayton Peace Accords, the settlement that had brought an end to fighting between ethnic factions. This involved enforcing the cease fire, supervising the marking of boundaries and zones of separation, the withdrawal of combatants, and the storage of weapons. But Peter did not care about the strategic significance of the mission. He had joined the army mainly to escape from his dead-end life, to channel his aggression, and to learn to use firearms properly. His experience in the Balkans taught Peter a few things. He never again wanted to experience the misery and desperation of the poor and downtrodden. He didn't want the course of his life to be determined by those who manipulated and abused their power and authority. And he knew that he wanted more out of life than what he currently had. To Peter, that meant having more money.

He became obsessed with money. He started gambling regularly with his fellow soldiers while off duty. He often won at cards, but it wasn't because he was a good player. He was lucky. His lucky streak gave him a false sense of confidence, so he organized regular card games and tournaments in the hopes of winning more, which he slowly did. Peter dreamed of returning to the United States with enough money to start a family and live a peaceful life away from the world's problems. The idea of having a home and a family appealed to him because he had never really been a part of one, at least since he was very young.

He finished his tour in Bosnia when his enlistment ended in late 1999. He hadn't liked life in the South, but outside of Georgia, the only other part of the United States he knew was New York City, so Peter found himself back in Brighton Beach soon after the New Year. While he was away, his Uncle Sergey had died of heart disease. Peter was determined to rise above the hopeless life he had first left behind and succeed on his own without subjugating himself to the city's criminal elements. It troubled him that he didn't have the skills to earn a large income. To succeed, Peter thought he needed to make the twenty grand he had won and saved while in Bosnia grow a little more. He never really knew how much he needed for a comfortable life and to support a family one day. He only knew that he needed more.

Then, the events of September 11, 2001, took place. The city was horrified, then saddened, then angry, and like the rest of the United States, prepared for war in Afghanistan. Al-Qai'da became a household name. Parts of the world that were unknown to most Americans were in the headlines: Afghanistan, Pakistan, and countries in Central Asia were on the news daily, and it seemed as if Americans were being introduced to the Eastern world again.

For Peter, these events could have just as well taken place on another planet. He cared little about world events. He struggled along as a construction worker, making ends meet and slowly putting a little money away as often as he could. Having grown up poor, he was very frugal, so he managed to save a little every month, but he did not think it was enough. Peter reluctantly decided to speed things up by doing what he did best, and that was playing cards.

Chapter Seven

Peter dragged himself off the sidewalk and started walking home, his body aching from the beating he had just received from Yury's men. He made his way through the darkened streets to the little house where he rented a small room from an aging babushka. He walked through the rusted metal gate and the small patch of grass the old woman called her garden and stepped into the old house. In his single room he fell onto the bed, in pain and with a sense of hopelessness. He covered his eyes with one arm and thought about his predicament. He had learned a lot about Yury Popov over the years. Popov was a shrewd businessman and was merciless in his dealings, two qualities that had enabled him to thrive in a town run by criminals. Peter knew that he would never be able to work off his debt. He would end up dead or in prison first. He concluded that he had no other choice but to escape Brighton Beach.

He looked around his bare room, for the first time thankful that he had so little. He wore his usual outfit; a pair of dark blue jeans, a plain white button-down shirt, and a light, black leather jacket. He threw the rest of his clothes and personal items into a large duffel bag and quietly stepped out of the house. The farther he walked, the faster his pace became, as newfound life coursed through his veins. He would only have this one opportunity to escape, and if he succeeded, he knew he could never return.

A yellow taxi idled at a corner under a streetlight, the driver sitting with his seat reclined and his eyes closed. Peter tapped the glass, startling the driver, who cracked his window an inch.

"The Port Authority bus terminal?" Peter asked, glancing behind him.

The driver twisted his face in annoyance and sighed. "All right. Get in."

At the bus terminal, Peter caught a bus to Fort Benning, Georgia, the only other place he knew. The ride was quiet and lonely. He left his youth behind him, as his only connection to the past, to his parents, and to his childhood, was now broken. Staring out of the bus window as cities, suburbs, and farmland passed by, Peter felt abandoned by the American dream. He was running out of options in a country that was supposed to have endless possibilities.

He had a friend from the army whom he could call, if the man was still around—Corporal Joseph Nelson, a fellow soldier from his time in Bosnia. Joseph was in logistics for the army and had procured supplies and equipment for the Third Infantry

Regiment. Peter and Joseph had had a mutually beneficial friendship while in Bosnia. Joseph gave Peter first choice on provisions, and access to hard-to-find equipment, in addition to an office in a warehouse for evening poker games. In exchange, Peter gave his friend a line of credit that was regularly cleared. They returned from the Balkans at the same time but went their own separate ways soon afterward.

At a rest stop in Richmond, Peter sorted through the slips of paper in his wallet and called Fort Benning's switchboard. Joseph Nelson, now Sergeant Nelson, was still listed. No answer. He reached a voice mail but didn't leave a message. Peter wondered if the sergeant would remember him, or even care to hear from him. A few hours later, he tried again from South Carolina. His old friend picked up the phone.

"Peter, how the hell are you?" Joseph asked excitedly. "It's been so long, I thought you were either a millionaire, in prison, or dead from liver disease."

"Well, you're not so lucky. I'm still alive and kickin'. Worse yet, I'm on a bus headed to Georgia. You gonna be around?"

"Yeah, I'll be around, but not for much longer," the sergeant replied. "I'm being deployed abroad. I'll tell you all about it. You're lucky that you reached me. When's your bus dropping you off?"

"At about 10:00 PM at the Greyhound station in Columbus."

"Damn. All right. I'll meet you there. What's with the short notice? You on the run?"

"It's complicated. Let's chat when we see each other. Apparently we both have a lot to talk about."

Peter and Joseph reunited at the bus station and went to Joseph's apartment. Once there, Peter told him about his last two years in New York City. Joseph's apartment was a single man's residence, and it was evident that he was moving out soon; all the furniture was functional, and there were very few personal effects on the walls or shelves. Boxes were stacked in the corners.

"So, I left my apartment and sneaked off to the Port Authority to catch a bus here. If I go back to New York, I'm a dead man," said Peter, concluding his story while opening the beer his friend had handed him.

"Jesus, man. You got yourself in deep over your head. This is just like you. I wouldn't have expected any less. You were never one to shy away from taking risks. So what did you hope to gain by coming back here? I doubt you're here to reenlist," said Joseph. He had thin lips and kept his thick, blond hair cut short.

"I don't know. I didn't think that far ahead. I suppose that's my problem. Then again, I didn't really have a choice. If I became Yury's footpad, I would probably end up retiring or dying in the same shitty neighborhood I was born in."

"Well, I wish I could help you. I'm being deployed to Karshi Khanabad, or K2, our new base in Uzbekistan. It's a logistics base supporting Operation Enduring Freedom in Afghanistan. I leave in four days. Sorry, man."

"Oh yeah? What's that place supposed to be like?"

"Dude, they say it's like Vegas, but better," said Joseph,

smiling. "The girls are incredibly beautiful, and they love Americans. Also, the dollar goes a long way there. It's a Muslim country, but you wouldn't be able to tell by being there, because everyone drinks, there are bars and clubs in Tashkent, and the girls dress like sluts."

"Yeah, so I hear. There are a lot of Uzbeks running around in my old neighborhood."

"Well, if you feel like getting out of the country for a while, you should come out there."

"I'm not sure if Uzbekistan is in the cards for me. I'm probably going to figure something out stateside."

"Suit yourself. You can crash here on the couch until I take off. There are towels, a pillow, and a blanket in the closet." The sergeant stood up. "I need to sleep."

"Okay. Thanks, man. I appreciate it."

Joseph shut off the lights and went to his own bedroom. Peter was exhausted. He hadn't changed or showered since he fled Yury's gambling hall. *Some mess I've gotten myself into,* he thought to himself, as he slipped off his hard leather shoes and stretched out on the couch. Peter considered doing construction work or becoming a security guard somewhere in town. He thought it would be a start until he figured out a new plan.

He woke up close to noon the following day. Joseph had already left for work. There was a set of keys on the coffee table. Peter took his time showering and getting ready. He rummaged through his black duffel bag, which contained everything he was able to throw together before he made his hasty retreat. Now it was everything he had to his name. He put on the same clothes he had worn the previous day and walked out of his friend's apartment.

The apartment complex must have been a motel once. All the doors in the two-story, L-shaped building faced the street or surrounded the open-air parking lot of the complex. Peter walked down the steps toward the management office, where there were a few soda machines and a pay phone outside, tucked into an archway. He flipped through the yellow pages—to the construction section—and began dialing phone numbers.

Two days later, Peter was standing in front of a foreman and a secretary inside a yellow doublewide trailer parked next to a small construction site.

"Yeah, I can hire you, but I can't give you any benefits, and I'll have to pay you in cash. Also, there's no guarantee how long I can keep you on board," said the overweight, red-faced foreman. "I'll also need a reference. If your previous employer tells me you work hard and know what you're doing, I'll pay you a couple of dollars more an hour. Deal?"

Because Peter had disappeared from his last job, he didn't know what kind of reference he would get. He knew, however, that he had been a good worker, so he gave the foreman his old boss's phone number.

Peter received a decent reference and started working the next day. Joseph left for Uzbekistan as scheduled. He told Peter that he could stay in the apartment until the end of the month, since the rent was already paid. The sergeant left a phone number in case he needed to be reached.

The construction job was less than ideal. The work was more grueling than Peter was used to. The foreman didn't have good equipment, and injuries were common. Peter ended each work day exhausted and then spent each evening drinking himself to sleep.

Chapter Eight

Yury walked through the street entrance and down the steps of the Soviet. A muscular, blond Russian with bad acne standing at the foot of the stairs nodded to Yury and said, "They are waiting for you downstairs, sir."

Yury kept walking toward the back bar. There was a haggard, brooding man with bloodshot eyes sitting at the counter, crouched over a small glass of vodka. An older, pencil-thin bartender smiled politely and said, "Good afternoon." Yury gave a curt nod and continued to the right of the bar and down the second set of wooden stairs that led to a door below. He opened the door and walked through.

He stepped into a busy, smoke-filled room crammed with rows of card tables, groups of men surrounding each. The men were of European or Slavic descent, in shabby clothing, but with handfuls of dollars. They yelled at each other and at the dealers with joy, and, just as often, with anger. But they were smart enough to keep their tempers to a non-threatening level.

Three heavy-looking men with sidearms nodded to Yury as he stepped into the basement gambling hall. The patrons quieted down, especially the angry ones, as he walked through the cement-finished basement toward the back wall. He approached a metal door with another armed man standing next to it. "I just let them in. Looks like good news," the man said as Yury entered the room and closed the door behind him.

He stepped inside his office. Two men in track suits were standing in front of his desk. Sitting behind his desk was his daughter Anna, who had blossomed to be a slender, striking woman with long, wavy, brown hair. She was dressed in a fitted red suit jacket with a very short matching skirt. She got up and moved to a seat to her right. The two men standing in front of Yury's desk stared at her slim, muscular legs as she moved to her usual seat when Yury was in the room. Yury sat in his old leather chair. He looked at the two men. "Well?" he said with some impatience.

Victor, wearing a blue track suit, was tall and bald save for the tufts of dark, curly hair on the sides and back of his head. He also had a protruding gut. Boris, wearing a red track suit, was equally tall but significantly more overweight, with matching bright red hair fashioned into a mullet. Yury trusted Boris. The man had always done what he was told and had never betrayed him. They had worked together for about twenty years, and Boris was now the most senior man on his payroll. "Good news, sir. We went to Ivanov's work to see where he was. The project manager was upset because he hadn't heard from him or seen him in days. Then he said five days ago he got a call from some man in Columbus, Georgia, asking about Peter's work history. He gave me the number of the guy who called," Boris said, as he handed a slip of paper to Yury.

"Columbus? I wonder what he's doing there," Yury said.

Anna shifted in her chair. "He spent some time in Columbus while he was in the army. He might have friends or an ex-girlfriend there," she responded matter-of-factly.

Yury leaned forward, rested his elbows on his table, and brought his fingertips together. Anna must have done some research. He looked at Boris and Victor. "Go find him. Leave tonight. We're lucky to have this lead. Trace the number and find out where he works. Ask around and find out where he lives. Discreetly. Then kill him. Bring back some proof that you completed your job."

"I'll go along to direct this," Anna said, leaning forward in her seat, making it clear by her tone that she did not want her father to object.

Yury looked at her and let out a deep, tired sigh. "I don't know about that, Annchka. Boris and Victor are competent. Let them handle this."

Anna's face reddened. "No. It was my idea to send them to Peter's old workplace. It was my idea to have him watched after you roughed him up, even though you didn't think it was necessary. If I had managed your affairs the way I wanted to, you wouldn't be in this predicament right now. Let me go with them and make sure this gets handled properly," Anna said.

Boris looked apprehensively at Victor. Yury had had a soft spot for his only child ever since her mother died when she was three years old. Anna was raised by a rotation of nannies and housemaids. Yury had neglected her for most of her childhood. He tried to make up for his neglect by putting her through college so that she could study business. He had checked on her regularly after she moved into the city and had discovered that Anna didn't have any real friends, just a group of girls who hung around her because of her looks and money. But they all feared her explosive temper. She used to have a few boyfriends who treated her poorly, which made her even more emotionally fragile. At first, Yury tracked down some of these losers and had them beaten, but he just couldn't keep up with all of them. Word also got around about what Anna's father had done to some of her boyfriends, and this made her situation worse. Boys started to avoid her. Her grades fell. At graduation, she didn't have the grades to get a respectable job that would finance the expensive lifestyle she had gotten used to. With reluctance, she had returned to her father to work by his side. He was surprised, since they were never close, and he believed, for good reason, that she resented him. Anna had grown into a hard, cold woman, and Yury knew that he was partly to blame for how she had turned out. He had welcomed her into his organization out of guilt. To his surprise, she embraced the duties he assigned to her. She was smart, and she knew what she was doing, but she was strangely overeager. He wished she was more patient.

Yury remembered Peter Ivanov. Boris had killed his parents a very long time ago. It was an accident, of course, and he had waived Sergey Ivanov's fees thereafter. The man hadn't paid a dime since. He had extended to Peter a large line of credit out of sympathy, but fifty thousand was a lot of money to let someone get away with. Many of the regulars knew that Peter owed the house a small fortune. Yury could only imagine what everyone else who had borrowed money would do if Peter was allowed to just disappear. He now considered his daughter's request to go to Columbus with his men. The job was straightforward, and Boris and Victor would do the dirty work. "Okay. You can go, but you need to stay out of their way. Let them handle this. You can supervise. Don't deviate from my orders without checking with me first. Understood?"

Anna knew the only answer he would accept was "Yes." She nodded and sat back.

"Do you want us to fly there?" Boris asked, not looking pleased about Anna tagging along.

"No. That will place you at the scene. Drive. I don't want any evidence of our hand in this." Then, a few seconds later, he turned to Anna and said, "Go tonight, get this done as soon as possible, and return immediately. Don't screw this up."

The next day, Anna was sitting in the back seat of a black Lincoln limousine in Columbus, Georgia. Through her large, dark Chanel sunglasses, she watched Boris, across the street, as he spoke to a man in overalls who sat eating a hoagie in front of a small construction site. Behind them, men were crawling around like ants on an almost-completed office building. More were lounging on a stack of bricks, chatting among themselves. Victor sat in the driver's seat, holding a burning cigarette out the window. He looked tired from the long drive—under the speed limit—from New York.

A few minutes later, Boris returned to the car and got into the passenger seat. He turned around with a satisfied look on his face. "I have his address, Ms. Popova. What do you want us to do?"

Peter was finally within her grasp. Anna had thought about him often over the years. He had disappeared soon after that fateful birthday evening so long ago. She had wondered what had happened to him and whether she would see him again. At first, Anna feared a run-in, but she developed confidence after growing up and joining her father's organization. Soon, she welcomed the opportunity to even the score. When Peter had showed up at the Soviet a month ago and she saw him at a table, she knew that her wishes had been answered. She just had to bide her time and wait for an opportunity. Now she had it. "Drop me off at the motel. Then go to his place and wait for him there," Anna said. "Try to be discreet about it. Once you have him, report to me. I want him alive, if possible."

Boris glanced at Victor in confusion, but he nodded in acknowledgment.

Twenty minutes later, Anna stepped out of the Lincoln at a small motel that accepted cash and didn't ask a lot of questions.

After she walked into her room, the Lincoln pulled away. She closed the door and pulled down the cheap flower-patterned window shades. Even though it was midday, she was exhausted. They had driven through the night, and she hadn't been able to sleep. Her small suitcase was sitting in the corner, but she decided not to unpack it. She sat down on the corner of her bed, pulled her cell phone from her purse, and began to dial her father, but hung up before the call connected. She didn't want her father to think that she was incapable of working without supervision.

Anna fell back on her bed and closed her eyes, wishing that her father took her more seriously. She knew that he had always wanted a son who could rise in the organization and to whom he could eventually hand the day-to-day management. Anna wanted to prove her father wrong and show him that he didn't need a son to manage his affairs. She wanted him to realize that the pressure he had placed on her mother to produce a boy was all for naught. Her mother had died because of his obsession with a male legacy. If she had to kill Peter to enlighten her father, fine.

Anna knew that the person she had become prevented her from making any real friends or having a romantic relationship. She had pushed away everyone who tried to get close to her. Her father refused to accept responsibility for her maladjusted development. She guessed that it was easier for him to blame others for her lack of friends or romantic relationships than himself. The truth was, her childhood had deformed her youth and hardened her against any warmth or passion.

* * *

Peter's muscles ached and his clothes were drenched with sweat as he exited the building under construction to get some fresh air. The midday heat did nothing to cool him down. He dragged himself toward a bench in the shade and collapsed. He looked at his raw hands before wiping the moisture off his face. For the last four hours, he had been hauling materials up five flights of stairs, but he felt as if he had been doing it all day. Footsteps approached him from behind. He turned around to see his foreman walking toward him.

"Is it your lunch break already? Make sure you keep track of your time," the foreman said as he sat down next to Peter on the bench. They sat in silence for a moment. "Hey, I forgot to tell you," he continued off-handedly. "Yesterday some guy called, asking if you were around. He said he was your Uncle Sergey."

Peter froze, and his face went pale.

"He told me that he'd try calling you at home, and asked for your home number. He said it was an urgent family matter, so I gave it to him. Did he reach you?"

Peter should have known better than to give the foreman his former boss's number. The boss must have tipped off Yury.

The pain in his muscles suddenly disappeared, and Peter bolted out of his seat. He ran from the site, ignoring the foreman who called after him. Peter went directly to his apartment, entering the complex through a side entrance and sneaking into an archway, from which he could see the front door of the apartment. It was ajar. He began sweating and wished he was armed. Fingering the passport and wallet in his pocket, he decided that the rest of his belongings had to be written off. He retraced his steps to the street and then caught a cab.

Peter checked into a Motel 6 on the other side of town. He closed the door to his room and sat down heavily on the bed. He stared at himself in the large mirror hanging on the wall. He would never be safe as long as he stayed in this country. Not that it mattered—he didn't have anywhere else to go or anyone else to turn to in the United States. The only remaining option was clear. Peter went to a cash machine and withdrew all the cash he could on his credit card. He went into the business office of the motel, which consisted only of a computer and printer, and booked a flight to Tashkent, Uzbekistan, leaving the next day.

That evening, he showered and then tried to sleep, unsuccessfully. In the morning, he went to a bank, wrote a check for about two thousand dollars to clear out his account, and was in a cab heading to the airport within an hour. At noon, he boarded the plane with only the clothes on his back.

Anna woke up to her cell phone ringing. Looking around the motel room, she realized where she was. She checked her jeweled Rolex—almost 8:00 PM. She had nodded off. She looked at the number on the phone. "What is it, Boris?"

"Ms. Popova, we've been at the apartment for hours. There's almost nothing here. It looks like the resident of the apartment moved out. There's a small duffel bag that looks like it's Ivanov's.

I also found an old bus ticket from New York to Columbus. I waited until 5:00 PM, but he never showed, so I sent Victor to watch the construction site. Someone told Victor that Peter took off without notice and hasn't been back since."

Anna slapped her hand hard against the nightstand, furious. "Find out who the tenant was and where he moved to. We need to know why Peter came here. Leave Victor at the apartment if you have to."

Anna hung up the phone and began to panic. Their only lead had just evaporated. She ran her fingers through her dark hair and squeezed her eyes shut. Knowing they would not get another chance to find Ivanov, she did not want to return to New York to tell her father that he had slipped away. She didn't want to fail at her first assignment. She thought for a few minutes and called Boris back.

"Yes, Ms. Popova?"

"Peter's on the run," Anna said. "Go to the airport and keep an eye out for him there. Send Victor to the bus terminal. If he decides to take a bus, he'll most likely go back there. I'll head to the train station," Anna said, trying to sound more confident than she really was. "He's going to leave, since he knows that we've found his apartment and workplace. He won't go back to either. If we don't spot him leaving Columbus by tomorrow evening, we'll start searching the city." Anna was taking a big gamble, but if all they did was wait in his apartment, he was guaranteed to get away. He could drive out of town, but there were too many places he could rent, steal, or borrow a car, and it would be impossible to determine from where with only three people. This was the best plan, and they had no other choice but to search for him, she reassured herself. If she returned empty-handed, her father would never let her forget this blunder, and her future in his organization would be limited.

"Understood, Ms. Popova. Should we notify Mr. Popov that we will not be returning immediately?"

"Let me deal with that. Just focus on accomplishing your tasks. Don't leave your positions until I instruct you to. If you find him, stop him. I don't want you killing him without me being present. If you can't stop him, follow him. Is that clear?" she asked with the same tone she had used to persuade her father to let her lead this operation.

"Yes, Ms. Popova. I understand," Boris said and hung up.

Anna reached into her purse and loaded her small, black Glock 26 pistol. She was slightly nervous but determined. Such an opportunity did not come often, and her future depended on accomplishing this task.

Yury felt alone in his office. He was trying to collect his thoughts and calm himself down, with little success. He sat with his palms pressed against his eyes, and wondered how events had come to this point. The assignment in Columbus was supposed to be a simple job. Peter Ivanov was just a kid who needed to be taught a lesson, and his death was to set an example for the other losers in New York who owed him money. He finally removed his hands from his face and looked up.

Standing on the other side of his desk were Boris and Victor. He wanted to shoot them both right now, but what lesson would that have taught the rest of his men standing around his office? They had only followed orders. Anna's orders. "So, tell me again what happened after Peter realized that you were looking for him?" Yury asked, with a mix of anger and perplexity.

Boris and Victor looked nervous. They were sweating, even though it was cool in the room. The other men standing against the walls in Yury's office fidgeted uncomfortably. They all worked for Yury, handling his dirty work, collecting his debts, and protecting his assets. Some did it out of personal debt acquired through gambling or drug use, others did it because they knew no life but a life of crime, and the rest were just stupid. None of them wanted to see Boris or Victor dead, but they would kill the two if Yury ordered it.

Boris spoke, as expected, because he was more senior, more responsible, and less likely to incriminate them both. "Ms. Popova ordered us to search for Ivanov. Victor was ordered to watch for him at the bus station, and I was ordered to look for him at the airport. Ms. Popova went to the train station. I waited at the airport all night and into the morning. I eventually saw Ivanov walk into the airport and proceed to a check-in counter. I decided to get in line behind him, and I heard the ticket agent confirm his flight to Uzbekistan. I walked away and called Ms. Popova to report what I overheard."

"And what did she say?" Yury asked with his thick, dark brows furrowed.

"She told me that she was on her way and asked me to call Victor to tell him to come to the airport. When she got there, she had her small suitcase with her, and she handed me another small bag that held her gun. She then told us that she was going after Peter. She said we were to return here and tell you about her plan. We offered to go with her, but she said no." Boris swallowed and looked down at his shoes. "That was the last we saw of her."

Yury's mind flashed back to his Red Army days in Uzbekistan. It had been so long ago. He found it strangely ironic that his daughter was headed to the country that he had escaped from twenty-two years ago. Was Anna out of her mind? What in the world was she going to do once she arrived in Uzbekistan? She didn't have a gun, and she was all alone. She wasn't ready to handle this on her own. Putting her in charge of this small task had been a big mistake. Yury couldn't blame Boris or Victor for what they had done. They were only following Anna's orders, just as he had instructed them to do. *Why didn't she check with me?* Yury wondered. *Why was she so hell-bent on catching Peter?* Yury forced himself to calm down and breathe slowly. He decided it was better to make the most of this unfortunate situation, since there was nothing he could do to contact her or turn her around. Maybe it would all work out. He was getting old, and if Anna could pull this off, maybe she deserved to take over in a few years. But she would need some help.

Boris shifted and asked uncertainly, "Do we know anyone in Uzbekistan?"

Yury didn't respond. He just closed his eyes and thought for a long time about this question.

Chapter Nine

The Manas restaurant in Tashkent consisted of a large dining room and two small yurts, the historical dwellings of the Kyrgyz people. The tent-like constructions were made by fastening heavy animal skins and cloth over wooden frames. The walls were cylindrical, the roofs conical. Inside each yurt was a low circular table at the center with large, soft cushions around it. The floors were covered with multicolored rugs, and an overhead lantern filled the interior with a soft, yellow light. Kurbon and Ravshan Usmanov sat next to each other, facing two middle-aged Kazakh men wearing business suits. Their shoes sat near the heavy, wooden swinging door, outside of which two large men silently guarded the entrance. A young Uzbek waiter stood nervously beside the guards, waiting to be called by the guests. The men could not make out the muffled conversation inside, and they didn't try to. Scattered elsewhere around the premises and the small parking area were three other men, who scrutinized the few patrons coming in and out of the restaurant.

For close to an hour, the Usmanovs and the two Kazakhs ate chicken, lamb, and beef *shashlik*—chunks of skewered meat grilled over coal, similar to kabobs, but fattier. They washed it down with two bottles of Russian Standard vodka. They made small talk, discussing the NATO military campaign in Afghanistan against the Taliban. More important, they noted that the conflict had increased the availability of opium. The Taliban had restricted opium production, but with their retreat, farmers in Afghanistan were again growing poppy plants, a far more lucrative product than other crops. Kurbon saw an opportunity to rebuild his faltering business, but first he needed to convince these Kazakh businessmen to join him in this venture.

Kurbon's hair had turned completely white since the night Alisher was arrested nearly two years ago. He also appeared unnaturally older and more tired. This evening, however, his face wore its most confident look. "I have been in the trafficking business for twenty-five years, gentlemen. With the exception of narcotics, I have moved nearly every conceivable product into Uzbekistan. I thrived and built myself a fortune. I have since embarked on legitimate enterprises and now own a successful coffee house and restaurant. However, the war in Afghanistan presents an opportunity that we can't afford to pass up. The profit margins are high."

One of the Kazakh men put down his fork and whispered, "Mr. Usmanov, you have only trafficked products into Uzbekistan. The heroin will need to travel to Kazakhstan. At least to Shymkent, just inside our border."

"I understand. This is a new challenge, but I can deliver. The borders—between Afghanistan and Tajikistan, and between Tajikistan and Uzbekistan—are porous. The border guards are the poorest in government service and can be paid off. I will bring the heroin to Shymkent and place it in your hands."

The other Kazakh man seemed a bit apprehensive. "This is a risky venture. If we agree to this, what exactly do you need from us?"

Kurbon raised his brows. "Yes, this is risky, but the rewards are great. I need a two hundred thousand dollar deposit from you to cover the initial purchase in Afghanistan. My part in this involves obtaining the narcotics and moving them from Afghanistan to Shymkent. In Shymkent, you will pay me one hundred and fifty thousand dollars after testing and taking receipt of the product. It will then be up to you to sell it in Russia, where you will likely receive a million dollars for the entire amount. Don't settle for any less. The value multiplies exponentially the farther north you travel."

The two Kazakhs looked at each other and seemed satisfied with the proposal, but they were obviously nervous. "Your offer sounds fair, but we will have to discuss this privately and get back to you."

Kurbon gave them his most winning smile. "As you wish."

After dinner, the Usmanovs left in Kurbon's old BMW.

Ravshan drove, while his uncle rode in the rear. Kurbon had given the vehicle to his nephew to keep as his own, with the understanding that he would have to drive his uncle around as needed. Ravshan had remained silent throughout the dinner with the two Kazakhs, likely afraid that he would ruin the deal by saying the wrong thing. He had grown noticeably more insecure over the last two years.

Kurbon turned around and glanced through the rear windshield, satisfied that the other black sedan with his four men was following closely behind. Kurbon no longer left his home without these bodyguards. Over the last year and a half, he had become a paranoid man. He expected reprisal from the families of the merchants who had been arrested. Recently, he had also begun to worry about other crime lords who would no doubt be unhappy to discover that the Usmanovs were entering the narcotics trade. And he feared that he was still on the NSS radar. He knew that there was nothing he could do about this particular threat, since they could arrest him at any time without cause, but having some muscle with him still made him feel safer. Ironically, Kurbon's paranoia extended to the men who protected him. They had originally been hired by Alisher. He knew that many of them had been saddened by Alisher's arrest, and he worried that the men might blame him for not having done enough to free their friend.

Kurbon's fortunes had taken a turn for the worse since that fateful winter evening. Once all the merchants who sold his contraband had been arrested, he had no way of offloading the merchandise that was coming in. He therefore had to stop doing business with his suppliers and traffickers. Many of them pulled out on their own after discovering what had happened to the merchants who had been tied to the Usmanovs. Kurbon's income took a nosedive, and his only income since was the meager revenue drawn from the tea house and the Café Three Oranges. He had used most of the money he had saved up to keep him and his nephew afloat. He was reaching the end of his savings and would soon be bankrupt.

Kurbon's proposal to the Kazakhs was his final, desperate attempt to rebuild everything he had lost. He was confident they would accept his terms. He just needed a plan to carry out his end of the bargain. He had made guarantees that he was actually unable to deliver. He could reach out to his extended family in northern Afghanistan to identify a heroin supplier and could probably convince one of his former Tajik traffickers to bring the narcotics just past the Uzbekistani border. But moving it from the south across Uzbekistan and past the Kazakh border was the challenge. All the traffickers who once worked this route no longer wanted anything to do with him. His current, meager staff was likely under government surveillance. And, most important, he did not trust them enough. They were not even aware of his attempt to enter the narcotics trade. He was uneasy about trafficking drugs and had never considered it during his better days, but his financial predicament had convinced him to put aside his scruples.

Kurbon's thoughts were interrupted by his cell phone ringing. He did not recognize the number, but it appeared to be from overseas. He reluctantly answered it. "Yes?"

"Hello, my friend. It has been a very long time." The voice was thick and raspy but somehow familiar.

"I'm sorry. Who is this?"

"It's Yury Popov. Do you remember me?"

Kurbon's eyes went wide with shock, and his heart skipped a beat. "Is this some kind of joke?" Ravshan looked at his uncle curiously through the rearview mirror.

"I've thought about you many times over the years, Kurbon. I always hoped you had fared well. Did you find a nice home for our three hundred Kalashnikovs?" Yury chuckled.

Kurbon's mind was filled with a mix of emotions. There was no doubt that the caller was his old friend. His former friend. "It can't be. I don't believe it. I don't know what to say. I thought you were dead. What happened to you?"

"I survived, like I always have. You seem to have done the same. Good for you."

"Where in the world are you?"

"In the United States. Can you believe it?"

"How did you get my phone number?"

"My current business in New York brings me into contact with many immigrants from the old republics. There are many people here from Tashkent. Many people with friends, or friends of friends, who are still there in your city. It took some work. It wasn't easy."

"So why are you calling me now, after twenty-five years?"

"I will be honest with you, my friend. I need your help, with something small."

Kurbon's was tempted to end the call at that moment. He didn't need some ghost from his past to make his life more difficult. "I'm sorry, Yury. I am going through a difficult time right now. My ability to do anything is very limited."

"Kurbon, I understand, but please listen to me. I just need you to do one thing. My daughter is traveling to Uzbekistan. Just speak with her. Meet with her once. That's all I ask." There was desperation in Yury's voice.

Kurbon wondered what this could be about. Maybe there was an opportunity here. One meeting couldn't hurt. "Okay. Have her call me when she arrives."

"Thank you, my friend. Her name is Anna."

Chapter Ten

Anna did not follow Peter to Uzbekistan. She was able to follow him to Frankfurt but then abandoned her efforts because she encountered two problems. Unlike the crowded flight from the United States to Frankfurt, the connection from Frankfurt to Tashkent was empty. When she arrived at the gate, there were only a handful of people, and Peter was easily recognizable given his muscular, athletic frame and the small indentation on the bridge of his nose that distinguished his face. Had she also entered the gate, she would have been discovered. She was not certain that he would have recognized her, but he had spent a considerable amount of time at the Soviet, so it was likely that he would. She was a difficult person to miss in that all-male environment.

She also had no plan for what to do once she arrived in Tashkent. She was on her own now, and the prospect of chasing Peter down in Central Asia made her anxious. She had been full of confidence and bravado while in Columbus with her father's men, but her confidence seemed to diminish by the hour. Her desire to impress her father had pushed her to follow through blindly with this task, but the long flight had given her time to realize that she needed help. It was very likely that she would lose Peter if she did not get on the plane with him.

She gathered her strength and decided to call her father. Now that she was halfway to Central Asia, and with her eyes on Ivanov, it was unlikely that her father would call it off. She found an airport pay phone and dialed him.

A surprised and upset Yury answered the phone. "Annchka, it's good to hear from you. I just finished speaking with Victor and Boris about your little adventure in Columbus. You have a lot of nerve chasing after Ivanov without my blessing. You're forgetting how little you can do without my resources and connections. Let this be a lesson on why you shouldn't decide on a course of action without first consulting with me," her father said. "If you were not my daughter, the consequences would have been severe."

Anna's anger rose with every word her father uttered. Calling him had been a mistake, she decided. Trying very hard to control her voice, she said, "I'm not calling you for a lecture. I'm calling to give you a status update. I have confirmed that Ivanov is headed to Uzbekistan. He's currently waiting at the gate here in Frankfurt. My problem is that if I also enter the gate, he will most definitely spot me, given that only a handful of people will be on the flight."

She could hear her father sigh on the other end of the phone.

"Good work, Annchka. Now come back home and let grown men handle this."

She nearly lost her grip on her emotions. "I'm not coming back. Either help me finish this job, or I'll figure it out on my own," she said in a strained, tight voice.

There was a long pause. "Well, my men did some digging, and we discovered that while in Columbus, Peter was staying with a friend named Joseph Nelson who is a sergeant in the army. This sergeant was just recently deployed to a U.S. military base in Uzbekistan. It's very likely that you will find Peter when you locate Mr. Nelson," Yury said wearily. "So, let Peter take this flight, and you catch the next one to Tashkent. Once you're there, find a place to stay and get in touch with me. I have a contact there who might be of assistance."

"Okay. I'll call you once I'm settled in Tashkent." There was relief in her voice. She didn't think her father would genuinely provide any help. But her problems seemed to have been temporarily solved, she thought happily. She hung up the phone and left the airport, optimistic about her prospects.

Anna caught the next day's flight to Uzbekistan, landing in the late evening. The airport in Tashkent had no skywalk for the passengers to enter the terminal, so they had to exit the plane onto a tarmac that was littered with green-clad, uniformed police. Passport Control was disorderly—no organized lines or intelligible signs to direct passengers to the appropriate border guard officer. Uzbeks nudged and pushed their way toward the front without any regard for the people around them. The border guards took a long time processing each visitor, given the necessity of documenting every detail of the visitor's passport, including other countries visited. This information would be cross-checked with their records to identify potential threats. This was one of the many steps the authorities took to safeguard against terrorism, espionage, unwelcome social and political influence, and dangers to regime stability. To add to the chaos, Anna had to wait for an hour before the luggage from her flight came through the carousel. No information was given regarding the cause of the delay, and she wondered whether the baggage handlers, or the customs officials, were searching the luggage.

Once she was outside the airport, dozens of men approached Anna and offered taxi services for an exorbitant fee. Not knowing any better, she paid twenty dollars for a two-dollar ride to the Uzbek government–owned Dostlik Hotel, which was recommended to her by an elderly German official who had sat next to her during the six-hour flight from Frankfurt. He also gave her a guidebook that he claimed had been helpful during his first few trips to Tashkent. Once in the city proper, she noticed signs of a foreign presence: American companies, such as Texaco, Newmont Mining, and Price Waterhouse Coopers were opening offices, and British American Tobacco was looking into establishing tobacco fields in the Samarqand area of Uzbekistan. The U.S. and German governments' diplomatic and military presence was also noticeable. Many of their official travelers were staying at new international chain hotels like the Intercontinental or the Sheraton. She ignorantly half-expected this country to still be in the Stone Age, with camels and yurts, but she soon learned that the Soviet Union had modernized Uzbekistan with a subway system, performing arts centers, universities and gray, depressing, Russian architecture. Even though Uzbek was the official language, Russian was still predominantly spoken in Tashkent, so she was thankful that her upbringing had given her a high level of proficiency. She had learned from the German official that the war in Afghanistan was drawing both security and economic interest from the West and that Uzbekistan was welcoming it. The country was shunning diplomatic and financial outreaches from its former colonial master Russia in exchange for closer ties to the United States and Western Europe. Many young people were even beginning to choose English as their second language instead of Russian.

Anna's excitement about making it into Tashkent in one piece was short-lived. She only expected to spend a few days in Central Asia, but the task of tracking Peter was proving to be difficult. In addition, she hated being dependent on her father's assistance. She called him from the hotel to say that she had arrived. He reluctantly gave her the name of a contact while alternately pleading with her to return and asking her to be careful. She got in touch with a Kurbon Usmanov, who said he would be willing to meet with her.

Two days after arriving in Tashkent, she was seated in a musky restaurant named the Café Three Oranges. Kurbon, accompanied by two meatier-looking men, approached her table and sat down across from her. He scanned her appearance, looking for familiar features. He never expected to be sitting across from Yury's daughter. He had always assumed that Captain Popov had not survived his trek to Pakistan. Yury's unexpected phone call had been difficult and uncomfortable. Kurbon had not been prepared for the call, and he did not know how to feel. Should he be angry that Yury abandoned him that night in Afghanistan? Kurbon partly blamed him for his brother's death, even though there was nothing Yury could have done to prevent it. They had both acted naively that evening. Either way, Yury was no friend. They had come together for a financial reason. That was all.

"Hello, Anna," Kurbon said to her from across the table. "How do you like Uzbekistan?"

"It's fine, thanks. But I'm not here on vacation, Mr. Usmanov. I would like to keep this trip short, so any aid you can provide would be appreciated," she said.

Her pleasant demeanor seemed forced and unnatural. Kurbon sensed that she wanted to get right down to business. *A true American,* he thought with distaste. She did not care to know him on a personal level but instead was looking for an immediate reward. He wondered if she had any knowledge of the history he and her father shared. "Well, Ms. Popova, I will tell you now that I do not owe your father any favors. So I'm not inclined to help you purely out of generosity." She did not respond, so he continued. "Your father was vague about what assistance you needed, so if you could elaborate, I would be better positioned to help you."

Anna looked uncomfortable and unsure about how to proceed. "Well, there's an American running around Tashkent who owes my father a lot of money. He's here to avoid paying. I'm here to track him down."

"And then what? If he doesn't have the money, paying you back will be difficult. What will you do then?"

"Then I will kill him. Our organization cannot reward him for running."

"What organization are you talking about?"

"My father's organization. He is a successful businessman, but he often has to deal harshly with people who refuse to stick to their financial commitments."

Kurbon was amused that his and Yury's lives had followed similar paths. They had both prospered and become businessmen of sorts. "How interesting," Kurbon said with a smirk. "Why didn't your father send someone more fearsome and less lovely for this kind of work?" Anna didn't respond. "So, this man's life is really of no value to you or your 'organization'? Only his money, or the example his death would provide?"

"I suppose that is correct," she said slowly, clearly uncertain where the conversation was going.

"Do you have a picture of him?"

She reached into her purse and passed him a photograph and a note containing some biographical information and a description of Ivanov's appearance. It also contained some information on Peter's friend Joseph. Kurbon read the note and studied the picture closely. "Peter Ivanov. He is Russian?"

"His parents were Russian."

"Were?" he asked, not really caring for a response. "Well, let me see what I can do. I can reach you at the Dostlik Hotel?"

"Yes. Thank you. But may I ask, what are you going to want in return? I don't like to make arrangements without knowing what I'm in for."

Kurbon thought for a moment. "Don't worry, Anna. If everything works out, finding Peter could be a win-win for the both of us."

While Anna waited for Kurbon to get back to her, she did some shopping, since she had never planned on being away from New York, much less being in a foreign country for so long. She found the women's clothing to be Western, but, surprisingly, more expensive than in the United States. By speaking to store clerks and customers, she discovered that prices were high because the majority of the retail items were bought overseas by Uzbek businessmen traveling as tourists. They would buy clothes and shoes in shops in Bangkok, Seoul, and Rome at full price and bring them to Uzbekistan for resale after marking them up more for profit. Even though many shops in Tashkent appeared to be chains of well-known brands, they were in fact not affiliated with the actual companies. Some suspected these shops to be fronts for money laundering.

Anna also noted that many women in Tashkent dressed in a

surprisingly risqué manner. The Russification of Uzbekistan had resulted in a certain level of promiscuity and alcoholism, unusual for a country where about 90 percent of the inhabitants were Muslim.

For a week, Anna returned to her hotel to find no messages. She hated being dependent on a man she did not know or trust. She spent her evenings fidgeting, thinking, pacing, and brooding. The fact that she was alone did not bother her. She had spent her entire life feeling and being alone. It was the possibility of humiliation and returning to New York a failure that disturbed her. Her father would see her as a nuisance rather than an asset, and his men would not respect her. She would be sidelined, her future as a leader in his organization uncertain. Then she truly would have nothing.

She received a phone call from Kurbon late one rainy evening. It rarely rained in Uzbekistan. The sky was normally clear and blue, but this evening it was dark gray, with heavy rain and strong gusts of wind. "How are you, Ms. Popova? Have you been well?" He spoke as if they were long lost friends, and he had not kept her waiting for a week.

"Fine. Do you have any news?" Anna asked, trying to keep her voice steady, but failing.

"Yes, I do," Kurbon paused, reveling in her dependence. "I tracked down our friend Peter. He is in Tavaksay Prison. Unfortunately, he was just thrown in there, so it's difficult to tell how long he will be in for. He severely battered a Ministry of Internal Affairs officer."

Anna's heart sank. This wasn't good. She could not stay in Uzbekistan indefinitely. "Are you sure?"

"Yes, I am. But don't worry, Anna. It's not so bad. The warden is a distant relation of mine, and I have a trusted friend imprisoned in Tavaksay. I have some ideas, but you need to have a little patience, and you have to trust me."

Anna wondered what this man was up to, and what his assistance was going to cost her. She did not trust him, but she didn't have options. She didn't appreciate being told to have patience, either. "What do you have in mind?"

"I will hand Peter to you, Ms. Popova. But it will take some time. Rumor has it that President Karimov will grant amnesty to small-time offenders. Peter will likely be released then. I will contact you when I have him."

Anna didn't like this man. She was sure he was up to something. But she needed him to get Peter. "Thank you, Mr. Usmanov. I will wait to hear from you, but please notify me immediately once he is released. Peter is important to my father and me."

"As you wish, Ms. Popova. You will know when I do. Enjoy the rest of your stay in Uzbekistan."

Anna put down the phone and looked out of her hotel window onto a darkening Navoi Street, a busy thoroughfare in the center of Tashkent. The rain was coming down hard and people were running for shelter, some holding paper or plastic bags over their heads. A large group of people with forlorn expressions were mashed into a single covered bus stop across the street, looking down the road for signs of their bus. Anna wondered what she was going to do now, and how long she would need to spend in this foreign land.

Chapter Eleven

Spring 2002

The inside of the prison cell was cool and a little wet. The moisture came from the heavy rain outside, which dripped slowly down the prison walls. The rain traveled through the muddy surface of the Tavaksay Prison grounds and the cracks on the walls into Peter Ivanov's cell. Luckily, the thin mattress on which he lay was dry, even though the floor had become a very thin pool of water. The cell wasn't completely underground. A small barred window near the ceiling was about one foot above ground level. He could see the dark sky and a dim light in the distance, which indicated the sun was beginning to rise. He stared at the streaks the raindrops left in the air as they raced down to the ground. Peter sighed with frustration. The heavy rain was beating against some kind of tin or aluminum surface, and the clatter was keeping him awake.

It was during these moments that he became despondent.

His life had slowly rolled downhill until it came to a stop in this small cell that he now called home. Just a temporary home, Peter reminded himself. The days and weeks went by slowly. Sometimes he felt unbearably alone and anxious about being held in a land with which he was unfamiliar. At other times, he felt a certain sense of relief, knowing that his past could not reach him as easily in Uzbekistan. But he didn't want to die in this cell. He often thought of dying, but not here, not in this way. So far, his prison stint hadn't really been that long. It just felt like an eternity. Being in the United States seemed like a lifetime ago.

Footsteps outside the metal cell door interrupted his thoughts and brought him back to the present. Two guards chatting with each other in Russian walked by, banging a baton on each door. Across from Peter on the other side of the room, his cellmate, Alisher Akhmetov, swung his legs over the side of his bed, sat up, and rested his head in his hands. He looked at Peter groggily and then at the wet floor and shook his head in disgust. Without saying a word, he walked over to the sink and began splashing water on his face.

Alisher began to put on his dark blue, single-piece prison uniform. Peter got up and took his turn washing his face. He began to cough painfully. The fit lasted for some time, then the coughing stopped, and he wiped away the tears that had welled up in his eyes. Peter's coughing fits had started three weeks into his incarceration. He suspected that he had tuberculosis, which came with any prison term in Uzbekistan. Alisher went about as if he hadn't noticed Peter's deteriorating health. It was likely that Alisher did not attribute the coughing to any ailment. Many

Uzbeks lived their entire lives with infections and diseases without seeking treatment, usually because of unaffordable healthcare or just plain ignorance.

Peter finished washing up and put on his jumpsuit. The two of them didn't talk much in the morning. For that matter, they never really talked much at all, so Peter knew nothing about his cellmate. There was a loud bell, and the single caged lightbulb on the ceiling flickered on. Over the next few minutes, voices from other cells increased in frequency and number. A second bell rang, and the heavy steel doors unlocked. They walked out of their cell and into a filthy, dimly lit hallway, to file into line with the rest of the inmates heading toward the large mess hall where everyone would have their breakfast.

Peter was an introvert, and, given the circumstances, he wasn't into making friends. As usual, he sat by himself after accepting his morning ration, and, as usual, Alisher sat with him in silence. Over the past month, Peter had figured out a few things about his cellmate. Like him, Alisher had no friends. The prison guards harassed a lot of inmates, but they left his cellmate alone. There were a few other inmates, however, who seemed to have it in for the guy. They gave kidney punches whenever they had the opportunity and occasionally spat in the man's food as he walked through the food lines. Alisher wasn't a big guy, but he fought back, though he could never successfully repel these attacks. If a prison guard ever witnessed the harassment, they severely beat the perpetrator, but never Alisher. Peter had the smarts to know that his cellmate was most likely connected to somebody with money or power.

Peter and Alisher reluctantly ate the flavorless porridge and the hard, brick-shaped bread they were given. They were soon crowded around on both sides by other inmates who wished to share their long table. The smell of urine and filth would have been overwhelming to a visitor, but the inmates had gotten accustomed to it. The slow murmur of conversation began to increase as the inmates woke up while they ate. Prison guards, batons in hand, slowly circled the large dining hall, eyes scanning for bad behavior. The table Alisher and Peter shared was somehow more crowded than usual, and they were crushed between men on either side. These men, like the majority of inmates, looked rough and smelled of stale sweat. Two inmates passing behind Alisher stopped to talk in Uzbek, a language Peter could not understand. Around the mess hall, Peter noticed a few scowling faces, some of which were directed toward him. He could sense a violent tension in the air; his sixth sense told him that something was wrong. He quickly lost his appetite.

To Alisher's left, a passerby accidentally spilled some porridge on a bigger, thuggish-looking Uzbek, who then sat up, grabbed the man, and began shaking him, forcing him to drop the remaining contents of the bowl on the ground. The clatter drew the attention of the men around Peter and Alisher, who began to yell and jeer. Most of the men around them stood up to get a better view of the fight, forming a virtual wall around the table.

A glint of light behind Alisher drew Peter's attention away from the melee. He looked across the table and saw a prisoner slip a small, crude blade out of his sleeve and into his palm. Peter recognized the man as one of the inmates who assaulted Alisher on a regular basis. To Peter's horror, the man with the blade began moving toward Alisher, who was nervously watching the fight, oblivious to the man moving toward his back. *This is not going to be good,* Peter thought.

Peter slapped Alisher's wrist with his wooden spoon to get his attention, and nodded toward his back. Alisher turned around, and his eyes went wide as he saw the man approaching him with the blade. He could only turn his head to look behind him because he was being squeezed by the men on either side of him. He could not turn his body to face his attacker. The man was five feet away and closing in. Alisher knew that he was going to be a dead man, and looked at Peter in desperation. Peter grabbed his bowl and tossed it at the assailant, covering the attacker's face and chest with hot porridge. The man screamed in pain and stopped to wipe his face with his sleeve. At that moment, Peter leaped onto the table, then jumped over the heads of Alisher and the men next to him, and grabbed the attacker's knife hand, twisting his wrist until the blade fell. Peter dropped to his knees to pick up the blade, but as he began to get up, a fist came toward his face. He felt a blinding pain, fell to the ground, and was soon trampled by the mob of prisoners around him.

Peter woke up on his rickety cot, finding himself once again in his small, damp cell. He had a piercing headache, and his face felt swollen and bruised. He lay staring at the cracked ceiling for a few minutes, trying to figure out why he was in so much pain.

"Here, take this," Peter heard in Russian from his left.

He carefully turned his injured head toward the voice. Alisher was reaching out with a wet towel. Peter took it and pressed it against his face. The morning's events came back to him, and he closed his eyes, thinking that he'd made a big mistake by saving his cellmate's life. He was now a marked man, and the men who had previously targeted Alisher were now going to come after him. *I'm not going to live to see the outside world,* he thought wearily.

"Thank you for your help this morning. I would be dead if it hadn't been for you," Alisher said.

"No problem," Peter responded. "What happened after I threw the porridge?"

"You were knocked out. Luckily, the prison guards were there, and they scattered the attackers with their batons. They carried you back here."

"Well, it must be my lucky day, then," Peter said, with sarcasm. A few moments later, he asked, "So, why is it that half the prison wants to see you dead?"

Alisher was quiet. He kicked his feet onto his cot and lay down. "It's a long story," he muttered. He said nothing for a minute, so Peter thought the conversation was over. Then Alisher continued.

"I used to work for a man named Kurbon Usmanov, who gave me the opportunity to make a significant amount of money by moving contraband into Uzbekistan. Traffickers would bring in all kinds of goods from China and the Middle East, and I would distribute them to merchants who would sell them on the black market. We had dozens of merchants in each bazaar, including the Chorsu and Caravan bazaars, two of the biggest in Tashkent. By helping Kurbon with his business, I was able to make a good income. But one evening our office was raided by the authorities. Luckily, the books on the incoming contraband, including the routes and the traffickers, were not confiscated because they were with Mr. Usmanov at the time. Unfortunately, the investigators were able to determine who the merchants in Tashkent were, so close to thirty people were arrested. When I was questioned, I took full responsibility and didn't give up the Usmanovs. But the authorities knew he was behind the entire smuggling operation, so they offered me a light sentence if I testified against him. But I didn't. So here I am in prison, along with all the merchants who were arrested. They are the ones who have been attacking me, and they staged the fight in the dining hall this morning. They blame me for what happened to them. Rightfully, I suppose."

"So, why do the prison guards leave you alone?"

"Because Kurbon knows that it wasn't my fault. He visited me here in prison right after I was incarcerated. He said that one of his men confessed 'under questioning' to telling the authorities about our office and the accountings located there. In any case, Kurbon paid off the prison warden to make sure that I am treated properly. He owes me for protecting him. I've been promised a nice bonus for my troubles and a senior position within his organization upon release," Alisher said with feigned confidence. "I'll just have to wait and see."

"Well, you seem to believe him. I hope it works out for you," Peter said, turning to face the wall and closing his eyes.

"What about you?" Alisher asked. "Why is an American here in an Uzbek prison?"

Peter was reluctant to tell his story, but he welcomed the human interaction. Alisher seemed like a harmless man. Having observed the rest of the prison population, Peter knew that his circumstances could have been much worse with a different cellmate. "I came to Uzbekistan about a month ago. I needed to get away from the United States for a while. My goal was to spend some time here, lay low, and make my money stretch for as long as possible. I had a friend here, but he was unexpectedly sent to Afghanistan soon after I arrived. So I was here on my own, killing time. During the first week, I went to a club named Ché Guevara, got drunk, and beat a man into a coma. I was arrested and thrown in here. The U.S. embassy is supposedly working on my release, but I'm not holding my breath," Peter said, speaking to the wall. "That's my story in a nutshell."

Peter considered the details he had left out, such as squandering his money on strip clubs and alcohol soon after arriving in Tashkent. To top it off, the man he had beaten into a coma was an off-duty Ministry of Internal Affairs officer. The U.S. embassy was having difficulty with Peter's release because the man was still hospitalized. Homeless, penniless, and on the run, Peter now had nowhere to go, even if he was immediately released.

Peter had also decided not to tell Alisher that he had defended him for purely selfish reasons. He knew that if Alisher was killed, he would have to share his cell with some criminal or psychopath, and under those conditions things might end badly for Peter. He considered himself lucky to have Alisher as a cellmate.

Over the following days, the two cellmates became close, mostly because neither of them had anyone else with whom to speak. Each spoke about himself and they bonded over the threat they now both faced from the inmates Peter had defended Alisher against.

During this time, one positive development took place. President Karimov, in honor of the Navruz holiday, was giving amnesty to women, criminals under eighteen and over sixty, foreigners, and first-time misdemeanor offenders. The president traditionally declared amnesty on a regular basis for various national and cultural occasions. Peter and Alisher were both included in this amnesty and were scheduled to be released within a week.

"Are you looking forward to having your freedom? You haven't gotten too accustomed to this cell, have you?" Alisher joked one evening, just before lights-out. "This place tends to toughen up even the softest people, but maybe you actually enjoyed the accommodations."

"I'm looking forward to getting out," Peter said, smiling. The truth was, even though he was looking forward to being out of prison, he was a little apprehensive about what he was going to do once he was released. He didn't have many options. He had thought about contacting the embassy, but the best they could do was put him on a plane back to the United States, a place he wasn't prepared to go back to. Peter didn't feel quite the same amount of enthusiasm the other prisoners, including Alisher, had expressed since the amnesty announcement.

"So, what will you do after being released?"

Peter had been afraid Alisher would ask this question. "I'm not really sure."

"Well, you can hang out with me if you intend to stay in Uzbekistan for a while."

Peter didn't respond. The lights went out in the cell. He looked out at the late-evening sky through the grilled opening near the ceiling. He was reluctant to jump on this offer. "Thanks, but I can't. I don't really have any money. The last thing you need is an additional burden."

"A burden? Peter, you saved my life. It's the least I can do, at least for a little while, until you get back on your feet. Don't worry about it. Money will not be an issue. Trust me," Alisher said, chuckling in the dark.

"Okay, I'll think about it. Thanks."

Peter eventually took Alisher up on his offer. It was his only opportunity, and he had to take it. The morning of their release, Alisher packed the few belongings he had. Peter didn't have anything to pack. Their cell door was opened and they were led through a few winding, dark hallways toward a processing office. There, an Uzbek guard in a spotless, starched uniform handed each of them a box and some papers. Peter opened the box and peered inside. It contained his leather coat, white button-down shirt, pair of dark blue jeans, leather boots, passport, and wallet.

He looked inside his wallet. Empty. He thought he had had a few dollars inside when he was arrested.

"Where is my watch?" Peter asked angrily.

The guard shrugged his shoulders and continued to read his newspaper.

"Come on. Let's go," Alisher said, pulling Peter by the elbow.

In a small room nearby they changed out of their blue prison jumpsuits and into their street clothes. They were then led outside and through three razor-wired gates. The air was a little crisp, but the sun was shining, promising a warm day. One of the guards standing by the gates waved. "Congratulations," he said smiling, flashing a set of yellow-stained teeth. "See you again soon." As Peter walked toward the waiting olive-green bus, the guard spat on his face.

Part III: Opportunities

Chapter Twelve

Peter and Alisher clicked their bottles of Baltika 3 together and smiled. They were at the Café Three Oranges. The place was dimly lit and filled with cushioned booths and cigarette smoke. A spinning disco ball hung over the small dance floor. A DJ stood behind a small booth next to it. On the dance floor were two young Russian girls who appeared to be in their teens, scantily clad in tacky leopard-print jackets, denim miniskirts, and knee-high velvet boots. They were dancing to an American rap song, gyrating erotically, but not to the beat, looking at their own reflections in the darkened windows. Only two other tables were filled, one with Uzbek men in drab clothing who were chatting closely around a table while toasting with shots of Russian vodka, and the other with a group of young, twenty-something Uzbek boys who were dressed as if they had just jumped out of an MTV video.

Alisher took a long gulp of his beer and chuckled. "It's nice to be free again, to drink beer, and to see women." They were both dressed in their old dusty clothes which appeared to have sat in a box in a crumpled state for too long.

"I feel the same way, and I only spent a fraction of the time you did in prison," Peter said, taking a sip of his beer. Baltika beer was one of the most popular beers in the countries of the former Soviet Union. It came in a variety of different brews. Baltika 3 was a light beer and probably the most popular. Baltika 0 was nonalcoholic, Baltika 6 was a dark stout, and Baltika 9 was the strongest. "So, who are we here to meet?"

"Ravshan Usmanov. He's my boss's nephew and acts as his deputy. Between you and me, he's an ass. However, if you want to do any work for Kurbon, you need to deal with Ravshan. I made contact with him right before we were released. I told him that I was indebted to you from our time in Tavaksay, and you were interested in doing some work."

Peter nodded. "Just like that, huh?"

"I vouched for you. That goes a long way here," Alisher said, still smiling.

"It goes a long way where I'm from as well." Peter wasn't necessarily looking for work, but he welcomed the opportunity to crawl out of the financial hole he was in. "I appreciate your help, Alisher, but only if it's not too much trouble. I don't want you going out of your way for me. I can manage just fine on my own."

"Peter, you need to allow people to help you once in a while. Stop being such a loner."

Peter knew that Alisher was right, so he shrugged off the admonition with a guilty smile. He *was* a loner, and old habits die hard. "What kind of work do you think Mr. Usmanov will have for me?" He was not excited about getting involved with a trafficking ring. But he was desperate and destitute, which forced him to go against his better judgment.

"I'm not certain. We have been out of touch for a very long time. But you shouldn't worry. I'll take care of you, Peter. I never forget people who have helped me through difficult times." Alisher had a newly youthful glint in his eyes that had appeared after he was released from prison. Freedom seemed to have a positive effect on him, Peter thought.

The bar door opened and an Uzbek man with dark, spiked hair and hip Western clothing walked in. He was dressed as if he was going out for the night and seemed to have expensive tastes. He saw Alisher and walked toward him with a smirk on his face. He and Alisher embraced and kissed each other on the cheek. "Good to see you again, my friend," the man said warmly in Russian.

"Good to see you as well, Ravshan-akka. I hope you're in good health. How is your uncle? Give him my warm regards," Alisher said equally warmly.

"He's doing well, and he's looking forward to seeing you. He wants you to come to his teahouse tomorrow afternoon, at 1:00 PM. You still remember where it is, don't you?"

"Of course. I'll be there," Alisher said. He gestured and said, "This is my friend, Peter Ivanov. I told you about him before we were released."

Ravshan had pretended not to notice Peter. Now he turned to Peter and gave a broad smile. "Ah, yes, of course. I remember. So, you're looking for some work? Well, I hope you're trustworthy, Mr. Ivanov. My uncle and I usually don't accept strangers into our circle without first doing some research. However, if Alisher has vouched for you, then that will do. My family is indebted to him. Come with Alisher tomorrow afternoon and my uncle will discuss everything with you. Until then, congratulations on your release," Ravshan said. He then reached into his brown suede sports coat and pulled out two large rolls of money. He handed a roll to each man. "Here. Enjoy yourselves tonight. Find a place to stay. I'll see you tomorrow." He squeezed Alisher on the shoulder, turned around, and walked toward the exit.

"Big thanks, Ravshan-akka," Alisher said to Ravshan's back as he was leaving. Alisher's warm smile faded to a frown as Ravshan exited.

As the door closed, Peter caught a glimpse of a black BMW parked right in front of the bar entrance.

"That was generous of him," Peter said, going through his roll of money. The roll contained approximately two hundred thousand Uzbek *soum,* worth approximately two hundred U.S. dollars.

"Don't be so quick to fall in love with him, Peter. He's not too happy about my release. It was evident by his disposition. And in regard to the money he gave us, chances are Mr. Usmanov gave more, but his nephew took a percentage," Alisher said, stuffing his roll into his pocket. He then took a long gulp of his beer, finishing the bottle. "Anyway, let's forget about that for now. We need to celebrate, and I know just the place."

"Okay, if you say so. Lead the way," Peter said, also finishing his beer. He wondered what Ravshan had done to upset Alisher so much. There was something there between the two that he wanted to figure out.

They stepped out of the bar. It was about nine in the evening and the weather was perfect—neither humid nor hot. They walked out to the main street and Alisher stuck his hand out. A Matiz, a small hatchback that could comfortably hold no more than four small children, pulled over to the side of the road. The Matiz was one of the many vehicles produced by Daewoo, the Korean conglomerate with a vehicle manufacturing plant in Uzbekistan. Most Uzbek vehicle owners either had a Daewoo or a Russian-made vehicle like a Lada. Only the rich or the connected were able to buy any other foreign-made car in Uzbekistan because of the high import taxes. Because of high unemployment, many vehicle owners acted as cab drivers on the side. Hitchhiking was a common and perfectly acceptable form of transportation, and one could go from one end of Tashkent to the other for the equivalent of two dollars.

They headed toward Amir Timur Square, where there stood a statue of Uzbekistan's ancient emperor riding on horseback. Peter looked out the window as the small vehicle made its way through the wide lanes, swerving in and out of traffic. *No one appears to follow the lane dividers here,* Peter thought. The roads were full of craters, and after a hard rain, it was impossible to tell which potholes were shallow and which could swallow a car whole. People would sometimes plant sticks in the deep holes as a warning to drivers to go around them.

They arrived at a large, colonial-style pink house with white pillars in front. "Bahor" was written in red lights over the entrance. They walked inside and up a flight of stairs into a large dining area with a high ceiling and a stage down front. Old Russian paintings hung on the floral-embroidered white walls, and well-dressed diners in Western attire were crowded around the tables. On the stage was a band, and an ethnic Uzbek man in a black suit was serenading a group of older women. The atmosphere was lively, and men and women were dancing around tables with their arms stretched out to either side, the traditional Central Asian dancing stance. "You're going to like this place," Alisher said as they were directed to a reserved table in front of the stage.

Alisher must have called in the order because almost immediately, a delicious lentil soup, rice, plates stacked with grilled lamb, beef, and chicken, and bottles of a sweet, red Uzbek wine called Qora Mavarid were set on the table. Peter had not eaten this well in months. Alisher ordered a bottle of vodka, and they shared shots throughout the meal while the male soloist sang in the background.

Eventually the lights dimmed, and a slow, jazzy techno beat

played through the loudspeakers. A fog machine shot smoke across the floor of the stage. "This is the best part," Alisher winked.

Through the stage entrance in the middle of the backdrop strode in ten beautiful, young, long-legged dancers, wearing thongs, with feathers wrapped around their arms and heads. With the exception of three Russian blondes, most of them had long, dark hair that they tossed from side to side as they danced provocatively. Peter could not believe that he was in Uzbekistan, an officially Muslim country. There was one girl in particular with soft, delicate, round features and a wide smile that grabbed Peter's heart. She was one of the lead performers. The girls went through a series of dances, but the belly dancing segment was the most arousing, as he watched her move erotically in a tight, shimmering black material that accentuated her curves. *Women in the U.S. could never move like that,* Peter thought. The show was seductive, corny, and shameless, and he loved every minute of it.

He forgot about his troubles. Yury and his men seemed so far away, and his memory of prison was like a fading dream. His eyes blurred, and his face flushed from the wine and vodka. Then it was the last dance routine, and all the girls were back on stage for their final number. He stared at his favorite performer as she pranced around stage in a transparent red genie outfit. She noticed Peter staring, but he did not care. She kept a smile on her face. As the girls exited through the stage door, she turned around and looked directly into Peter's eyes, again smiling. And then she was gone. The dancing had lasted a full hour, but he wished it had continued all night.

The lights brightened, and the audience applauded. Peter looked at Alisher and said, "You were right. That was my favorite part of the evening."

Alisher laughed. "Welcome to Central Asia, my friend. The night's just beginning."

Alisher dropped eighty thousand *soum* on the table. Not bad for an endless supply of food, wine, and vodka for two people, especially at a high-end establishment. Peter's vision began to spin as he stood up. His tolerance for alcohol had dropped while in prison. Alisher grabbed him by the arm and directed him down the stairs and toward the exit. They stepped outside into the cool air, and once again Alisher stuck his arm out. An old, Soviet-era Russian vehicle with torn seats and a withered, geriatric driver pulled over. Alisher pushed Peter in and followed him into the car. As the car began moving, Peter rested his head on the window and looked up. The clear sky was ink black and filled with small stars. He blacked out as he stared into the universe.

Peter woke up with a throbbing headache. He slowly opened his eyes. Above him was a white ceiling with a wooden fan spinning on a low setting. He was in a bed with soft, mustard-colored sheets. He lifted his head and looked past his toes to take in his surroundings. There was an old television with dials and worn-looking dark wood furniture in the room. The place was clean, but it didn't look as if anyone really lived in it. There was a doorway to a bathroom, and another door with a bolt lock and a peep hole. Was he in a hotel? He didn't remember checking into one. He looked to his left, and in front of his face was a mass of long, dark hair strewn all over the pillow. He looked under the sheets and saw that he and the woman were naked. His stirring woke the woman, who lifted her head and turned toward him. She was a young Uzbek who was attractive, but not the woman he had hoped she would be. She smiled shyly, with sleepy eyes and then snuggled up close to him. She gently rubbed his chest and then slowly slid her hand down. This could be fun, he thought, and closed his eyes. But seconds later there was a short knock on the door, and Alisher walked in. The girl gave a yelp and sprang to her feet, holding up the sheet to cover her naked body. Peter could see her bare behind and noticed that she didn't have the definition the dancers from Bahor had. *Oh well,* he thought with amused pleasure. Alisher came farther into the room, raised his eyebrows, and smiled. "Peter, it's getting late. We have a meeting today, remember? Get dressed and meet me downstairs." He reached down, grabbed Peter's clothes off the floor, and tossed them onto the bed. "Oh, and you're paying for the rooms." He walked out and closed the door behind him.

The Uzbek girl looked at him and pouted her lower lip, dropping the sheet to display her nude body. "I think that's my cue to get dressed," she said in Russian in a light voice before picking up a black miniskirt and a loose blouse off the floor. Her clothes were on in ten seconds. She faced Peter with one hand outstretched and another on her hip. She smiled and said matter-of-factly, "You owe me forty thousand."

Shit, a prostitute, he thought. His conquest had been too good to be true. While struggling to recall how the previous evening ended this way, Peter dug out his wallet and looked inside. The roll of money was lighter than he remembered. He counted out forty thousand *soum* and tossed it on the bed, hoping it had been worth it. The girl picked it up, stuffed it in her blouse and walked out, gliding her hand along Peter's thick neck and shoulders as she walked out the door.

As the door closed, Peter began another round of heavy coughing. He covered his mouth with his hand, and when he withdrew it, his palm was stained with blood. His symptoms were getting worse, and he needed medical care. Peter stared at the palm of his hand for some time, collecting his thoughts. *Once I have enough money, the first thing I'm going to do is go to a hospital,* he promised himself. He then wondered what would come out of the meeting with the Usmanovs and how much he could trust Alisher. Since his release, everything seemed to be working out a little too well for him.

The taxi ride to the teahouse was painful. The strong sunlight beating down on Tashkent was not helping Peter's hangover. The roads were teeming with people. Among the pedestrians and cars were carts being pulled by donkeys, slowing traffic. Every few blocks, a man or woman with a small table holding cigarettes and soft drinks sat on the side of the road, selling to motorists who didn't have time to stop at a store. Men without work, with nothing to do or nowhere to go, squatted along busy streets, watching aimlessly as life passed them by. Heavy-set women in traditional, multicolored dresses and bright orange jerseys, completely oblivious to oncoming traffic, swept the roads with wide straw brooms, forcing vehicles to honk and swerve around them. Tashkent seemed foreign yet comfortable to Peter, and he wondered how long this city would be his home.

The taxi pulled into a residential neighborhood, and soon passed through a gate into a wooded area. "We're here," Alisher said.

Peter and Alisher stepped out, and the small, compact taxi turned and left. They were standing in a clearing next to a small stream with man-made stone banks on both sides. The clearing was surrounded by the knotted and misshapen mulberry trees that were common in this part of the world. A small, one-story green building with a large patio stood at the edge of the clearing. On the patio, and scattered throughout the clearing, were large, knee-high, square-shaped platforms, about seven feet long on each side, resting on stumpy wooden or metal legs. These raised platforms were called *topchans* in Russian, and were meant for relaxing and lounging while snacking or having tea. The platforms were covered with cushions and pillows. On the *topchans* that were scattered throughout the clearing, old men sat or lay in the shade, facing each other in a circle. They were enjoying naan and tea or playing dominos on short tables set in the middle of the *topchans*. Alisher gestured toward a *topchan* and said, "Mr. Usmanov is over there. He owns this *choihona* and spends a lot of time here. If you ever need to find him, there's a good chance that he will be here until sundown."

They started walking, and a few of the men resting on *topchans* looked up at them curiously as they passed by. Peter noticed men in sports coats who appeared to be bodyguards scattered around the clearing, standing stone-faced, watching them. Two stepped up to pat them down. Finding nothing, they returned to their positions. Ravshan was sitting on a platform, looking less festive than the previous night, but still well-tailored in a gray sports suit with a jet-black shirt. Next to him sat Kurbon, who observed Alisher and Peter approach with an amused smile. When the two guests reached the Usmanovs' *topchan,* Ravshan nodded his head, while his uncle broke into a wide grin. "God has blessed me with two gifts today. An old friend who has always been loyal and a new friend who wants to work for me," Kurbon said in eloquent Russian with his arms extended up into the air. "Sit down and break bread with me."

Alisher put his right hand on his chest and bowed slightly. "Kurbonjon, I have looked forward to seeing you again for a long time. I'm glad to see you in such good health. This is my friend Peter, who I spoke to you about."

Peter tried to imitate Alisher's hand gesture and bow. "It's a pleasure to meet you, sir. Thank you for seeing us."

Kurbon appeared to be pleased with the gesture. "The pleasure is all mine, Peter. Now sit."

Alisher and Peter sat cross-legged, adjacent to each other along the two unoccupied sides of the *topchan.* The elder Usmanov poured green tea into two matching small cups from a blue porcelain pot with a white design representing cotton plants and handed one each to Peter and Alisher. An old, hunched man in a multicolored robe approached them and set down a large plate of *plov*—yellow rice garnished with chickpeas and small pieces of beef. Like nearly every dish in Uzbekistan, the *plov* was saturated in oil. A favorite national dish, it was eaten on every occasion, including a normal day's lunch. Another plate with large round pieces of bread also appeared. Kurbon, Ravshan, Alisher, and Peter served themselves—in that order.

Kurbon set his fork down and looked warmly at Alisher. "I want you to know that I'm very sorry for the time you spent in prison. You were caught and convicted for work you were doing for me, and you never betrayed me. For that, I will be forever grateful. As a reward for your loyalty, you are promoted as of today to be my third in charge, second only to my nephew. We can discuss your salary later, privately."

Peter noticed that Ravshan's eyes had slowly widened as his uncle spoke, but he tried to hide his surprise with a grin. Clearly, Ravshan hadn't been told, much less consulted, about this decision. "Congratulations, Alisher. You deserve it," he said flatly.

Alisher looked moved by this promotion. "Thank you, Kurbonjon. Working for you has been my pleasure. You will not regret this promotion. Thank you."

"No need to thank me, Alisher. You earned it. There are very few people I can trust, and fewer still who have the brains and responsibility to help me manage my growing enterprise." Kurbon paused for a moment to chew and swallow. "And what about you, Peter? What brings you to Uzbekistan and to my little *choihona* here in Tashkent? I do have to admit, I have never been approached by an American for employment. I'm honored. The economy must really be in poor shape back in the United States," he said, chuckling.

These were the questions Peter was afraid Kurbon would ask. Until now, he had eaten and just listened to the conversation. He was observing Kurbon Usmanov carefully, trying to determine whether he was the kind who was loved, despised, or feared by his men. So far, the jury was still out, but Kurbon's having rewarded Alisher for his work was a positive sign. "Well, I wanted to see the world, so I followed a friend here, but he was sent to Afghanistan soon after I arrived, and I was sent to prison for beating an MVD officer. I could return to the United States, but I would return a poor man. Alisher thought you could help me earn some money before I leave. I'm just looking for some work before I return to the U.S. for a fresh start. I'm not interested in having a career here in Central Asia. But if you have any opportunities, I would be grateful. I have military experience, I've done some construction, and I'm good at cards," Peter replied, not knowing what else to say.

Kurbon smiled. "Unfortunately, I do not need any help with construction. Even if I did, with the amount you would want as compensation, I could just as easily hire a hundred Uzbeks. And, I'm not currently in the gambling business, even though it's worth thinking about in the future. You see, Peter, I'm not inclined to hire people on a short-term basis. I like to keep my business interests within as small a circle of people as possible." Kurbon paused and assessed Peter. "However, Alisher has vouched for you, and I understand that he owes you a favor. So, I'll let you do one task for me. But before I divulge any details, I need to know whether or not you are willing to do it." Kurbon paused for a moment, studying Peter's reaction. He grew serious. "I need you to transport eighty kilograms of narcotics for me. In return, I'll give you sixty thousand dollars."

Peter hadn't expected Kurbon to get right to the point. Fear and excitement gripped his throat. This was no simple task. Eighty kilograms was about one hundred and fifty pounds. Being caught with that amount of drugs would shorten his life, to say the least. He would be lucky to receive a trial. If caught in transit, he could just as likely be shot and thrown in a ditch, the narcotics confiscated and resold by some corrupt border guard or security officer. On the other hand, he could recover all the money he had lost in New York. With sixty grand, he could repay his debt or start over again somewhere else. The money provided a lucrative opportunity at a time when Peter thought all hope was lost. He struggled with this decision for only a few moments. He knew that without a large sum of money, the next few years of his life would be difficult as he struggled to stay afloat, slowly making small amounts of money while skipping from country to country, hiding from Yury. He didn't have the patience or the fortitude to eke out a living, constantly on the run from his debts. He would be killed before his dreams ever materialized. Therefore, the opportunity Kurbon presented was tempting. He swallowed his fear and asked, "How long would it take for me to pass the narcotics on after I took possession of it?"

"What you are really asking is how long you would be

responsible for it. A few hundred miles. About fifteen hours of driving at the most, fewer if you're fast. I wouldn't recommend it, though. Better to stay under the radar and not draw attention. You don't want to be pulled over." Kurbon again waited for an answer. Alisher and Ravshan also sat, looking at Peter. Was that sympathy Peter saw in Alisher's eyes?

Peter again collected his thoughts and nerves. "Okay, I'll do it."

Kurbon smiled and appeared to relax. "Good. Understand that I don't offer these kinds of opportunities to everyone. Eighty kilograms is no small amount. I'm placing a lot of trust in you because I'm confident you can do it. You have an advantage, Peter. As an American, you will not receive the scrutiny that a typical Uzbek or Russian would. Go to the Tajik border, take possession of the narcotics, and store them in the car we give you. Then drive them to Shymkent, just past the Kazakh border. That's it. Do that, and you'll be sixty thousand dollars richer."

"Okay. Sounds easy," Peter said, trying to smile and look confident.

Kurbon nodded and leaned back. "It's fitting that you will be doing this task for me. The U.S. invasion of Afghanistan has increased the narcotics flow through Central Asia to Russia and Europe. Narcotics trafficking is now very profitable, more so than ever—because of you Americans," he said, chuckling to himself. "Ravshan will contact our people in Tajikistan and Kazakhstan and tell them to expect you." Kurbon poured more green tea into everyone's small cups. He then raised his cup and said, "To new friends, and new opportunities."

Peter, Ravshan, and Alisher raised their cups. "Good luck to you," Alisher said seriously from across the table. Peter hoped he didn't need it.

Chapter Thirteen

Peter decided to leave Kurbon's teahouse on his own. He wanted to walk off the hangover and spend some time thinking about the decision he had just made. He couldn't get over the fact that he had just agreed to traffic heroin. This was a new low for him. He found it ironic that his parents had escaped the Soviet Union to find a better life, but he had chosen to travel to Uzbekistan to join the criminal underworld. He doubted his parents would have been amused by the irony, but Peter made a promise to himself that he would not let their sacrifice go to waste. He would do something better with his life. Something honorable. Someday, but just not yet.

As he walked, his thoughts drifted elsewhere. Before he embarked on this potentially dangerous assignment, there was one thing he needed to do.

* * *

Madina Aliyeva did not find fulfillment in her work. Every day was the same. She woke up most mornings wanting to stay in bed and escape back to her dreams. Her parents were proud of her, and they were absolutely confident that she would pick her future husband from dozens of successful bachelors. But, more than marriage, she wanted to see the world and, more important, leave Uzbekistan. With so few options for work and pathetically low wages, it would be impossible to live a comfortable and fulfilling life here. She did not want to get by—barely—year after year. She knew that her beauty wouldn't last, and once it was gone, her life would no longer be as valued. She was in the prime of her life. If she was going to pursue her dreams, she had to find the right man who could provide the means to escape. This was easier said than done. Many of the foreigners were transient, and the locals getting rich in Tashkent were doing so because they were connected to government officials or were involved in organized crime. Madina didn't want anything to do with either.

She forced herself to get back to reality and focus on today, because today she was late for work. She traveled via tram to the center of town. The trams rode on a rail located in the middle of wide roads, separating the opposing lanes of traffic. The trams traveled slowly, frequently broke down, and were at the mercy of vehicles that cut across their path or drove along the rails to pass slower moving vehicles on the road. But it was cheap and allowed her to use her hard-earned money to help her family. Until she came across a magic pot of money, she would continue to endure this frustrating commute.

She got off the tram at Amir Timur Square and walked toward the Bahor Restaurant, where her fellow dancers had already started practicing for the evening performance. She was headed toward the side gate, through which the employee entrance was located.

"If you walk any faster, you'll get whiplash when you stop," she heard a man's voice say behind her. She hadn't passed anyone, nor had she heard anyone approach, so she was startled. She spun around, ready to shoo off the likely stalker but froze when she recognized him.

It was the man she had noticed the previous night in her audience. He was handsome in a rugged sort of way, and the slightly crooked nose and muscular build gave him a hard edge that she liked. He and his friend had also spent a lot of money, which was a good sign for a potential suitor.

"Oh, hi," she said, trying to appear nonchalant. She turned and continued walking, but slowly.

"So you remember me?" Peter asked, quickening his pace to walk next to her.

"You were at the show last night."

"I knew I made an impression," he said, smiling.

"You're very confident," she said, unable not to smile in return. "Your Russian has an accent. Where are you from?"

"I'm from the United States."

Madina was pleasantly surprised, and it showed on her face. "You're a long way from home. Why are you here?"

Peter hesitated, stumbled over his words, and then said, "I'm here on business. An import-export business."

"What do you import and export?" she asked skeptically.

"Well, I export carpets out of Uzbekistan and import them into the United States."

"Oh, have you found a lot of nice carpets here?"

"I haven't yet, but I'm hoping to." Peter paused for a moment. "You are a talented dancer, by the way."

"Oh, thank you."

"However, I think you could use a few pointers."

Shocked, and not knowing whether to be insulted, she asked, "Oh, really?"

"Sure. But it just so happens that I am a very good dancer, and I could teach you. But you first have to go out to dinner with me." Peter smiled.

Madina was approaching the gate and needed to go in. But she was interested in getting to know this man. "I don't even know your name."

"It's Peter. Peter Ivanov." He extended his hand.

She took it and said, "I'm Madina." Peter held on to her hand for a moment.

"I need to go inside. I'm late."

"I'm going out of town for a day or two—to buy some

carpets—but when I return, I would like to see you," he said and finally let her hand slip away.

"Do you have a cell phone?"

"Yes," he said, and pulled it out of his pocket. She grabbed it out of his hand and punched in her number. She returned the phone to him. "Now you have my number. Call me when you get back, but not after 8:00 PM. I'm dancing then."

"Great. You'll definitely hear from me soon." Peter said with a broad, boyish smile. Madina simply nodded, turned around, and walked through the gate. He watched her walk away and then moved to the street and flagged a cab. When he turned around to face the oncoming traffic, he noticed a car parked on the other side of the street a short distance away. The occupant, a male driver wearing a hat and dark sunglasses, was observing him.

Alisher and four of Kurbon Usmanov's men were dining and drinking on a *topchan* at the outdoor teahouse. Peter had left an hour before, to rest before leaving the next morning on his assignment. Alisher was celebrating his new promotion with the men, all of whom he had known prior to his prison sentence. All four were uneducated footpads, having served the same function for Kurbon since Alisher hired them years ago. They would most likely spend a good part of their lives providing general muscle, making sure that money was collected and ensuring that contraband would flow through Uzbekistan, then suffer early deaths or go to prison. Alisher pitied them, but he did not feel guilty for bringing them into this line of work. They and their families were much better off. It would have been wrong for him not to have offered them this opportunity. He had grown up with them and worked at Chorsu bazaar with them. They were miserable back then.

So Kurbon is now in the narcotics business, Alisher thought with trepidation. It was probably a development that could have been foreseen, given the Usmanovs' previous line of work. If Kurbon was able to transition into moving heroin, they all stood to make a significant amount of money. Alisher's new salary was already at least ten times that of the average Uzbek. He wondered whether Peter was ready for the narcotics business. The American had definitely grown up in a criminal environment, had guts, and could fight. But did that translate into successful smuggling?

Alisher's vision was blurry. He and the men around him had been laughing, reminiscing, and taking shots of vodka since Peter left. Ravshan had been invited to join, but had passed, leaving the teahouse soon after Peter did. *Good riddance,* Alisher thought. He could tell that the other men were equally happy that the younger Usmanov had gone. Ravshan never spent time with the men he supervised. He looked down on them, used them as tools, and cared nothing for them. Ironically, he would most likely take the reins once Kurbon retired. Alisher had lost almost two years of his life in prison, and he had lost his love for the Usmanovs. It pained him to think that Ravshan, the man he knew had betrayed him, would one day take charge of Kurbon's businesses. Alisher shook his head, trying to clear his mind of these thoughts. Everything had been going well for him since his release. He wanted to enjoy this moment and not think about the past or future. His curiosity about Kurbon Usmanov's guest kept drawing his attention, however.

Across the open clearing, Kurbon shared a *topchan* with a striking, brown-haired woman. She had arrived a few minutes earlier, in fitted, dark blue jeans and a cropped, brown corduroy jacket. She had walked to Kurbon's platform after identifying herself to one of the bodyguards but without waiting for approval, or allowing anyone to check her belongings. As if she owned the place. The man who had first questioned her passed Alisher and mentioned that she appeared to be American, even though she spoke some Russian. Alisher wondered what a young American woman was doing here in Uzbekistan speaking with his boss. He couldn't help but wonder if she was somehow connected to Peter.

Alisher liked Peter, and felt a little guilty about having manipulated him into working for Kurbon. Ever since the Usmanovs had visited him in prison and ordered him to become close to Peter and lure him to the teahouse with an opportunity to make a lot of money, Alisher had wondered what Kurbon had up his sleeve and what Peter's role was in it. Alisher had staged the prison scuffle and pretended to befriend Peter because Kurbon had asked him to, but in the process he had grown to like him. Peter had genuinely tried to save his life, and there were not a lot of people who would have done the same. In this business, everyone was looking out for himself.

The woman was speaking animatedly with Mr. Usmanov and was clearly upset. But by the end of their twenty-minute conversation she appeared to have calmed down. She stepped off Kurbon's *topchan* and walked rigidly out of the clearing, back in the direction from which she had arrived. Kurbon made eye contact with Alisher, smiled, and raised his small tea cup in a toast. Alisher responded with the same gesture, and returned his attention to his comrades. Whatever Kurbon was up to, Alisher did not like it. One thing was for certain: he was not going back to prison.

Anna returned to the Dostlik Hotel fuming. The meeting with Kurbon had not gone well, but she was not surprised. Instead of handing Peter over, or providing information on his exact whereabouts, Kurbon had sent him on an errand, and promised to deliver him only after he returned. To her great annoyance, Kurbon had simply referred to their earlier conversation.

"You said yourself that his life meant nothing to you. Only his death or his ability to repay you was important. So, I gave him the opportunity to earn the money he needs to repay you. If he is killed while completing this task for me, then you can take credit for his death back in the United States."

Anna was irritated by his response for two reasons. First, it delayed her departure from Uzbekistan, a country where she had already spent more time than she ever imagined. Second, he had deceived her and not fulfilled his promise immediately. Luckily, she had gone by her instincts and not trusted him.

Back in the hotel, Anna walked down the hallway to her room and opened the door. Victor sat idly on the edge of the bed, scanning television channels. He quickly stood up as she walked in. Victor and Boris had arrived four days ago, sent by her father after he discovered that his contact might not live up to expectations.

Anna dropped her small purse onto the office desk and sat down heavily on its matching chair. "My meeting didn't go well. Kurbon deceived me, as expected. He's now sending Peter on some errand. What's Boris up to?"

"He just called. He spotted Peter leaving the same teahouse you were at with the Usmanovs. He's tracking him at a distance as we speak."

"Good. Get ready to meet up with Boris. We are going to follow Peter and finish this job on our own."

Ravshan sat at a corner table of the Efendi Turkish restaurant. His plate was filled with chunks of grilled beef, rice, and *lahmanjun*, a thin, round tortilla covered with minced meat, chopped parsley, and spices. He slowly picked at his meal, lacking an appetite. He was sitting on the restaurant's outdoor patio, which was filled with families and groups of men enjoying dinner in the cool evening air. Ravshan was the only person eating alone.

He hadn't eaten much since Alisher was released. He had passed on dinner with Alisher because the thought of celebrating the promotion of the man he had sent to prison sickened him. Alisher deserved the promotion he received. He spent almost two years in prison without selling out the Usmanovs. Ravshan knew that he couldn't say the same for himself. His uncle had never discovered his betrayal, but he was forever anxious that it would come to light. He had had no contact with Salim, the NSS officer, since their meeting that one winter night. He thought that was for the best. Ravshan had naively trusted him and, as a result, been rewarded with a more thorough investigation that had cost the Usmanovs their business. He never wanted to see or hear from this man again. He hated Salim.

He wondered if Alisher suspected him or knew that he had gone to the NSS. If Alisher did, then Ravshan's life, or his already tenuous relationship with his uncle, was in danger. Alisher was a connection to a moment in his life that he was ashamed of. Alisher was now back with his men, surrounded by friends, and had more authority and resources at his disposal. Even Kurbon loved him. There was nothing to stop Alisher from undermining his authority. Ravshan did not want him around. Nothing good would come out of it.

The next morning, Peter sat in a fairly new silver Nexia, a Daewoo-built version of the Honda Civic for Uzbekistan. Nexias were everywhere, popular among the middle class. The car was parked in a small garage in a residential area of Tashkent. Kurbon's men made the preparations for his trip the previous day. He had been contacted this morning via the new cell phone he had been given at the teahouse. Peter had also been given a Makarov pistol with two full magazines, each holding nine rounds, and nearly one thousand dollars worth of *soum* to cover expenses, including any snags he might encounter. Otherwise, all he had were his U.S. passport and the clothes with which he left prison.

Alisher and three of Kurbon's men were in the garage with Peter. His former cellmate was standing next to the car with the other men, who were checking the engine and fluids. The men finished their inspection, closed the hood, and walked away. Once they were out of earshot, Alisher leaned into the passenger side window.

"Be careful, Peter. Don't trust anyone, and finish this job quickly. The longer you are out there, the greater the chance something unexpected could happen. So, try to rest as little as possible, and don't draw any attention to yourself." Alisher paused to make sure Peter was listening. "After you have the drugs, stash them in the specially fitted compartments under the seats. Also, there are workmen's tools in your trunk. There is paperwork in the glove compartment that says you are traveling to Surhandarya province to provide advice and equipment to a building site. A similar set of papers, also in the glove compartment, says the same about your trip to Shymkent. Many Uzbeks travel daily to Shymkent in order to find work in Kazakhstan, so pick up some migrant workers when going to Shymkent if you need to. You have the map in the glove compartment with your pickup and delivery points marked. And you've been instructed on what to do when you make contact with both parties, right? Do you have any questions?"

"Not really. It sounds pretty simple, as long as everyone knows that I'm coming." Peter sat looking straight ahead at the closed garage door. He then turned to Alisher. "Did you know that Mr. Usmanov would ask me to do this?"

A guilty look came across the Uzbek's face. "He's new to the narcotics trade. He's an impatient man, and he wants his organization to grow. Drugs are big business and almost a must if you want to rise to the top. When I worked for him before, we were involved in other contraband, but I'm not surprised that he's now into narcotics. It's an easy transition. So, yes, I suspected that you would be asked to do something related. However, I didn't know specifically what. I'm sorry I wasn't able to give you some kind of warning before he offered you the job. But don't worry. You'll be fine."

"Congratulations again on your promotion. I think the future is looking bright for you," Peter said, meaning it. He was glad his friend was doing well. Alisher already appeared younger and more energized since his release. He no longer had that tired look around his eyes. He deserved to do well, after doing time and keeping his mouth shut. Kurbon's men returned and opened the garage doors.

"Finish this, and your future will not look so bad, either," Alisher said. "Anyway, good luck. Call only if you have problems. Otherwise, stay off the phone."

"Okay. I'll see you soon," Peter said, forcing a smile. He started the ignition and slowly pulled out into the street. He began winding through the neighborhood, swerving around large craters and groups of children playing in the streets. He reached Halklar Dustligi Road, a major thoroughfare heading south to the city border twenty minutes away. Peter had a nervous lump in his stomach and felt completely alone, not for the first time in his life. He was literally traveling down a road from which he couldn't turn back. He had committed the moment he left Kurbon Usmanov's teahouse. In order to calm his nerves, he began to think about what he could do with the money that he would earn by completing this task. He daydreamed of a comfortable life back in the United States, which still felt like home, even though he had no friends or family there. He wondered if anyone would miss him if he died in Uzbekistan.

Chapter Fourteen

As Peter drove out of Tashkent, he thought about what he wanted out of life. He had no grand ambitions or goals. He only wanted the ability to buy the things he desired and live his life to the fullest. He dreamed of enjoying his days with a small circle of friends and a beautiful woman whom he trusted and who would accept his sordid past. He just needed some money for a fresh start. Everything would be different then. Everything would be better. He promised himself that he would strive to make a simple, honest living after putting this distasteful job behind him. He knew he was better than this.

He settled into the drive, accepting his current task as a necessary step in the right direction. His destination lay approximately eight hundred kilometers south of Tashkent, in Surhandarya province, which shared borders with Afghanistan and Tajikistan. Peter's rendezvous point was in a small town named Uzun, a few miles north of Termez, once the southernmost point of the USSR.

His directions were clear: Drive south toward Termez until you enter Surhandarya. Soon after going through the provincial border checkpoint, turn left at the first roadside bazaar in the town of Uzun. He then had to turn right onto a dirt path, immediately after the only street lamp on the street. His suppliers would meet him at the end of the path. With these directions in mind, Peter drove out of Tashkent, hoping that nothing would go wrong so he could return to Tashkent in one piece. No one would have considered Peter a coward, but he never sought out danger or trouble for thrills. He just wanted an easy life, and a quick fortune was his means for getting it.

His drive south was a visual feast. He passed cars and vans bursting with produce, with cabbage, melons, and potatoes piled high and visible through the windows, the drivers barely fitting into their seats. He drove past fields of wheat and cotton and orchards of apples. The farther he went, the more conservative the dress became. Women wore skimpy Western clothing in Tashkent, but as he drove south, he noticed that they were more covered, their clothing more traditional—ankle-length, single-piece gowns. The dresses were colorful: yellow, red, blue, and green patterns decorated the garments. The women's hair was often pulled back and their heads wrapped in scarves. Most Uzbek men wore dark slacks and a button-down or polo shirt. Many also wore flat, square-shaped, black skullcaps. Due to Russian influence, the great majority of Uzbek men, both urban and rural, were clean-shaven.

When Peter began his drive, the terrain was flat, with pastures on both sides. Within a couple of hours, the ground became hilly, with green fields as far as the eye could see. Peter saw a person standing in a pasture two miles away because the landscape was devoid of trees or shrubbery. Flocks of sheep moved in loose clusters, roaming the grassy hills with shepherds, often adolescent boys, watching over them on donkey-back, stick in hand. After Samarqand, the terrain became mountainous. The road curved more often and more drastically, traveling up and around snow-capped mountains, with small streams formed by the melting snow trickling down the sides. After six hours, the greenery disappeared, replaced by yellow, orange, and red patches of earth. It reminded Peter of pictures he had seen of the American Southwest.

The drive was not entirely pleasant. It was obvious to him that the countryside was poverty-ridden. At one point, he drove past a rally, where a group of women were protesting gas and electricity shortages. Their signs indicated that corruption and bureaucratic ineptitude were to blame. The women prevented traffic from passing along the road, so green uniformed militia officers beat them back with batons.

Peter drove through no fewer than ten security checkpoints, each manned by a handful of the same green-uniformed militia officers. The farther from Tashkent he traveled, the more scrutiny he received. At first, officers lazily waved through his car and others, if not completely ignoring them. Once he passed Samarqand and entered the mountainous Kashkadarya province, however, militia officers randomly motioned cars to pull over to the side and searched the trunk, checked identification, and inquired as to the driver's destination. At the Surhandarya border, the road was barricaded, and every car was searched and every driver questioned. Peter was nervous—on the return drive, he would be loaded with heroin. But neither he nor the interior of the car was searched, and his story wasn't questioned, so he tried to remain calm. This assignment was stressful, but sixty grand for two days of work wasn't so bad.

After driving for approximately nine hours, Peter finally crossed into Surhandarya province. It was 5:00 PM. He was tired and his muscles ached from sitting for so long. To his relief, he saw the roadside bazaar—the first landmark that Alisher had mentioned—after another twenty minutes of driving. Men and women were toting loaves of naan, baskets of vegetables, and raw meat on hooks, all of which appeared to be covered with dust from the road. But he was famished, so he pulled over, purchased a few meat-filled *somsas,* three bottles of water, and a bottle of cheap vodka. He then continued following directions until he passed through a large brick archway, indicating that he was entering the town of Uzun. After another three hundred meters, he spotted the streetlight and turned onto the dirt path immediately after it. Overgrown trees shaded the path. It dead-ended in the distance at a brown farmhouse.

Peter cautiously exited his car and looked around. The farmhouse was made of mud, dilapidated, with high grass and weeds on all sides. He walked around to the back of the house, finding a yard with a bare *topchan.* Peter looked inside the single-room house, and, to his relief, found it empty, except for a few rusted pans and clay pots. An outhouse sat a few yards away, set into the woods. Finding nothing suspicious, he made himself comfortable on the *topchan* and stretched his legs, looking at the view that lay before him.

The rear of the house faced a stretch of small fields with a row of single-story, flat-roofed square farmhouses running behind them that were identical to the one he was in. Behind the string of farmhouses were low grassy mountains, through which ran the Tajik border. As the sun fell behind the mountains and shaded the fields, the inhabitants poured out of the farmhouses to use the last few hours of daylight for work in the fields. The men and women wore traditional clothing, while small children played around them. Peter lay on the platform watching them work and play for the next few hours, until the sun disappeared completely. He admired their simple life and wondered if they ever aspired to more or wished to see other parts of the world.

He ate the oily, room-temperature *somsas* and pulled out the Makarov pistol and examined it closely. The Makarov was the pistol of choice within the former Soviet Union, and it was still used throughout Central Asia. Unfortunately, each magazine could only carry nine rounds, many fewer than Western pistols Peter had fired while in the army. The Makarov was accurate for only about thirty meters. He tucked it away, into the back of his pants, hoping he wouldn't need to use it. He opened his bottle of vodka and took a long gulp.

He thought about the upcoming meeting with the narcotraffickers. The Usmanovs had already paid for the heroin, so he was not expected to pay the traffickers for it. He hoped they knew that. He was simply to take possession of the narcotics. Peter's understanding was that Kurbon was to receive payment for the heroin in Tashkent once the delivery had been made in Kazakhstan. This meant that Peter would not see a dime of the money until he returned to Tashkent. He didn't like the arrangement, because the Usmanovs could leave him with nothing or change the terms of their agreement after he had completed the delivery. He didn't know how these Central Asians operated, but if he was double-crossed, he intended to put his pistol to good use. He could draw on a lot of courage when there was nothing more to lose.

Soon it was dark, and he knew the traffickers would arrive any moment. Not wanting to be surprised, Peter stepped away from the *topchan* and walked into the trees, keeping his car and the front door of the farmhouse within his line of sight. There he sat on the ground against a tree and waited in the darkness. No firm time was set for when the traffickers would arrive, so with each passing hour, Peter became more restless and impatient, and worst-case scenarios began racing through his mind. What if there had been a miscommunication and they expected some form of payment? What if a passerby or the owner of the property appeared? What if the traffickers had no intention of passing the heroin, but instead planned to kill him and make off with the narcotics? He shook off these thoughts and took another large gulp of vodka. He was tired, so he leaned his head back against the tree and closed his eyes, feeling the alcohol warming his body. He listened to the crickets and the frogs, and the light wind blowing through the trees. He began drifting off to sleep, picturing Madina dancing. He wished he could magically fast-forward to the time when this job would be over. He told himself that he would never again take on a job like this.

Peter awoke with a start, hearing rustling along the path that led to the farmhouse from the main road. Panicking, he wondered how long he had nodded off. He immediately began to sweat, wondering what he might have missed. He noticed three human forms, with large humps, approach his vehicle and examine it. The darkness made the forms look like turtles walking on their hind legs. They split up, one staying by the car, another going around the house to the *topchan,* the third going to the front door. Peter took a deep breath and swallowed hard. The moment of truth had arrived. He crawled slowly toward his vehicle through the trees, staying in the shadows but keeping his eyes on the farmhouse. Eventually, the two figures by the farmhouse disappeared from sight. Taking advantage of the moment, Peter approached his vehicle. The figure by the vehicle moved slowly, hesitantly, and seemed focused on the Nexia. When Peter was ten feet from his vehicle, the figure standing by his car heard the movement and turned toward him. His heart racing, Peter quickly stepped toward the man with his hands to his sides, ready to draw the pistol behind him. He realized then that he was facing a startled young kid. The boy appeared to be in his late teens, was covered in dirt and dust, and had a large canvas pack on his back. "Good evening," Peter said softly, slowly holding up his hands.

"Hello," the boy said nervously. He then turned toward the house and gave a birdcall. The two figures left the farmhouse and quickly approached Peter—another young boy and an older man, both appearing equally dirty and worn. There was a family resemblance about them, and they smelled like earth and sweat. The man approached Peter and awkwardly extended his hand.

"Good evening, sir. Do we know anyone in common?" The man used broken Russian. His skin, like that of his sons, was darkened and hardened by the sun. This family was Tajik, and men like him and his sons lived in the border regions. They were poor, lived under difficult conditions, and trafficked in contraband, including narcotics, in order to get by. The great majority of the people involved in the narcotics trade in this area smuggled out of necessity.

"Yes, I think we do. He is a *paxtakor,*" Peter said. *Paxtakor* was the Uzbek word for cotton picker, the password Alisher had instructed Peter to use. "Do you remember his name?"

"His name is Mahmud." This was the response Peter was hoping for. He gave a small sigh of relief, but the trafficker and his sons still appeared nervous. Their eyes were constantly scanning the dark forest. Peter's guard went up instinctively. It was eerily quiet.

"Okay, let's load what you have into my car." Peter walked to the Nexia and opened the back door. He grabbed the flashlight from the passenger seat and switched it on, shining it on the interior of the car, watching the traffickers from the corner of his eye. He felt around the edge of the floorboard, and, finding a small lever, pulled it. The back seat cushions flipped up, revealing a large compartment. "Put everything in here."

The older man nodded to his sons to start unpacking, while he continued to look back and forth from Peter to the tree line. Peter shined his flashlight onto the two boys, who settled their large packs on the ground and began undoing what appeared to be an endless series of strings and cord. They reached into their packs and began pulling out brick-sized, brown paper-wrapped packages. One boy passed the packages to the other, who settled them in the hidden compartment. Peter was restless. These boys could not move fast enough, and this assignment could not end soon enough.

After what seemed like an hour, the boys wrapped up their now smaller bags and strapped them onto their backs. Peter counted eighty packages total. The father and sons seemed impatient to leave, slowly backing down the path toward the mountains. "Wait," Peter commanded, walking to his vehicle, aiming the flashlight away from the small family and into his car. He shined his flashlight into his hidden compartment, which was now packed with small brown packages. Peter stuck his finger into the creases of one package and worked it slightly loose with his fingers. He felt a thin plastic bag, so he tore a small hole, and dabbed his finger into the clumpy substance. He pulled his finger out and rubbed the powder against his gums. He didn't really know what he was doing, but he did not want the traffickers to think he was incompetent. He had no intention of driving all the way to Kazakhstan with eighty kilos of flour. The substance didn't taste like sugar or flour, so he nodded in satisfaction. The father and his sons continued to inch away down the path. As Peter moved the beam of his flashlight from the compartment back to the three ragged traffickers, he caught a movement along the dark tree line past the opposite side of his car.

Before he could isolate the movement, muzzle flares brightened the area, blinding him. Peter threw himself on the ground and scooted behind a tire, his military training taking over. The traffickers shrieked and started running toward the farmhouse and the fields beyond. Peter's nightmare scenario had begun. What had been a quiet night was now filled with muffled gunfire and the sound of the Nexia's windows and metal frame breaking from a steady volley of automatic weapon fire. Peter drew his weapon and pointed at the tree line from over the hood, sure that the traffickers had double-crossed him. He was stunned when the father and one of the boys were hit with gunfire as they attempted to flee. Their bodies shook as multiple rounds hit them. Their screams cut through the air, and then the gunfire stopped. The remaining son was sprinting, about to round the farmhouse and disappear into the darkness. Peter heard a short burst of muffled fire from the tree line, and the shadow of the boy dropped to the ground.

Peter heard footsteps approach his car from the opposite side. He darted into the trees in a crouched position, keeping the car between himself and the attackers. The muzzle flares indicated that there were three shooters. Peter zigzagged about twenty yards, dropped to the ground, and hid in the tall grass, facing his vehicle and the men approaching behind it.

Three figures dressed in black with their heads wrapped in dark scarves stepped out of the trees holding AK-47s. One figure walked to Peter's side of the car and aimed his assault rifle into the woods, slowly scanning the darkness for his target. The other two inspected the silver Nexia and then jumped into the front seats. One of the men began working on hot-wiring the ignition. The man behind the steering wheel fumbled with his head scarf and tore it off, revealing an older Uzbek face. Peter focused on his profile but did not recognize him. The man had salt-and-pepper hair and a dark mark on his left temple that might have been a scar or birthmark.

Fear gripped Peter's throat. Complete failure was within sight. He was on the verge of losing half a million dollars of heroin. He was also on the verge of being killed. He needed to decide what to do. Quickly. He aimed his Makarov at the figure searching the forests for him. If he fired, he would draw return fire. On the other hand, if the men drove away with his vehicle, he would have a lot to account for. He knew from growing up in Brighton Beach that he would be considered ultimately responsible for the fate of the heroin, and if he returned to Tashkent empty-handed, he would suffer terribly. He had no choice.

As his Nexia came to life and the engine revved, Peter carefully aimed his pistol at the chest of the standing figure. He fired three quick shots, and immediately rolled two yards to the left. The figure fired a shot wildly into the air as he fell. The man with the scar hesitated in the car for a moment, seeming to consider whether to help his fallen comrade, but he stepped on the gas instead, reversing quickly down the tree-covered path. Peter ran to the edge of the path and fired the remaining six rounds at the car. He heard the windshield shatter, but the car continued on, backing all the way onto the main road and disappearing into the night.

Peter ejected the empty magazine and loaded another while staring down the dark path. A wave of dread and hopelessness came over him. He ran a hand through his short, dark hair, pinched his eyes shut, and held back a scream. Tears welled up in his eyes, and his throat constricted. He could not think of any other time in his life when he had felt so low and helpless. His entire life seemed to have been a series of poor decisions, one leading to the other. He looked down at the pistol and considered pointing it at his own head. There was nothing left for him now but a life of fear, poverty, and loneliness. He needed to run. He had to flee this country. He wiped the tears from his face and looked at the bodies around him.

He walked toward the motionless masked figure on the ground. The dead man's AK-47 lay beside him. He inspected the weapon and saw that the magazine was empty. It was useless to him. The figure was not moving, but Peter shot another round into him to make sure he was dead. He pulled the mask off and examined the corpse's face. The man was Uzbek, appeared young, and had an athletic build. The ground around him was dark and wet with his blood, which drained to the side of the dirt path and into the grass. Peter crouched down on one knee and searched the man's black athletic pants. Nothing. His hands shaking, he fumbled through the inside of the man's dark jacket, blood making his fingers sticky. From a pocket he pulled out a dark leather bifold, but suddenly he heard movement behind him, so he stuffed it in his jeans and spun around.

It was one of the young boys, struggling on the ground. Peter walked over to him and stared down at him. The boy was gurgling blood, his eyes wide open in horror. He looked at Peter and held his gaze, pleading silently for help. He was lying on his back, trying to take his pack off, but he was too weak to do so. His wounds looked bad, and his clothes were stained crimson. Peter's heart ached for him, because there was nothing he could do to help him. This kid's death would go unnoticed, his short life insignificant in the course of world events. Peter wondered if his own death would be equally pointless, forgotten immediately by history. He considered shooting the boy, to put him out of his misery, but he only had eight rounds left and didn't know what else was in store for him this evening. The robbery and gunfight had hardened his heart. Tucking his Makarov into the back of his pants, he walked away from the dying kid to the back of the farmhouse. He looked out at the dark fields, which looked like the ocean at night, with a few dim yellow lights from farmhouses floating in the distance like buoys. The mountains behind the distant farms blended into the black sky, making them indistinguishable. Peter sprinted into the dark fields without looking back.

Chapter Fifteen

Anna, Boris, and Victor followed Peter out of Tashkent, not knowing where he was heading. They were driving a stolen black Lada, a Russian-made sedan with no frills. Anna wore black fitted dress pants with a light, black cashmere sweater, while the two men were in their usual track suits. They were armed and ready to take Peter down the moment an opportunity presented itself. But none of them knew what to expect. Following Peter at a distance had not been too difficult, because during many stretches there was only light traffic. Bumper-to-bumper traffic was unheard of in Uzbekistan, even in the major cities.

The drive was quiet. Although Boris and Victor were close, there was really no friendship between Anna and her men. She had no interest in chatting about her personal life, and she didn't care to hear about theirs. She wanted Boris and Victor, as well as the rest of her father's men, to see her as a capable leader who should be respected, but she was not comfortable with building rapport. She felt that these men would be less likely to respect her if they knew her on a personal level. Behind her self-satisfied confidence and sense of superiority, she felt that there was nothing very special about her. By remaining mysterious, she hoped that Boris and Victor would not catch on. During rest stops, when she saw the two men laughing and bantering, however, she wished she were included in the comradeship.

After a seemingly endless drive, they watched Peter turn off the main road and into a small village. They did not follow him in, knowing that they would be detected easily. Instead, from the main road they watched his Nexia travel down a street before turning out of their sight.

Boris, clearly the leader of the two, turned around from the passenger seat to face Anna. "Now that we know where he is, let's wait until he is settled and comfortable before we move in. When it's dark, there will also be fewer people around. After driving all the way here, I doubt he'll get back on the road immediately. For now, we can go on foot to confirm his location and determine who he might be with."

Anna thought about Boris's suggestion. She could not think of anything better and knew that he had more experience with these things. Nevertheless, she wished she had been the one to think of the plan. "Okay, that sounds fine. I'll wait here. Come back and let me know what you find."

The men exited the car and set off on foot down the road that Peter had turned onto from the bazaar. She watched them walk away. She thought about going with them but did not want to appear incompetent during surveillance.

Victor turned back to look up the road at the waiting Anna. "That was a tough drive. It's too bad she's with us. I hate babysitting, and we could do this better without any supervision."

Boris smiled, glad that Victor had said what he was thinking. "As long as we make her feel important, she won't micromanage and will leave the field work to the men. The last thing I want is for her to get us killed."

"She *is* a pretty girl, there's no doubt about it," Victor whispered, smirking. "Very easy on the eyes."

"She's a nutcase, that's what she is."

"Well, I'm glad you're with me, Boris. I can't imagine being stuck with her alone on this."

"I agree. Listen, let's split up. Once we get to the path that Peter turned onto, you stay on the road, and I'll go in a bit to see what he might be up to." Victor nodded and dropped back, allowing Boris to walk ahead.

Boris reached the mouth of the wooded path and looked down it. The path was shaded from the bright sun. In the distance, he could see Peter's parked Nexia. He pulled out his pistol and jumped off the path and into the woods. Carefully stepping through the thick foliage, he slowly walked in the direction of the vehicle, constantly scanning the trees, the path, and the car for any movement. Once he neared the vehicle, he saw a small farmhouse. He listened intently but heard and saw nothing. *Peter must be behind the house,* Boris thought. He decided to turn back. He found Victor waiting aimlessly on the road and relayed what he saw to him. They then walked back to their black Lada. As they did, they noticed curious faces peering at them through windows. It made them nervous.

Boris liked having Victor around. The man wasn't very smart, but he was loyal, fearless, and never said "No." He still remembered his initial meeting with Victor, four years back, when they were first assigned to work together. They were sent to New Jersey to take out a Ukrainian immigrant who had started selling ecstasy in Brighton Beach without clearing it with Yury or any of the other bosses. Boris and Victor killed the Ukrainian in his apartment as he watched TV. Before torching the apartment, Boris came upon twenty thousand dollars the dealer had stored in shoeboxes in his closet. He took half and gave Victor the other half. It was one of the perks of doing Yury's dirty work.

They had gone outside and headed toward their car, only to discover four men leaning against it. The Ukrainian's friends. Boris and Victor split up before they were seen. They planned to walk separately and meet up again in Brighton Beach. They could always come back for the car some other day. Ten minutes after they split up, Boris found himself walking through a darkened warehouse district. Deserted. Not a soul or cab in sight. He rounded a corner to find a Beretta pointed at his face by two of the Ukrainian's friends. They searched him and took his gun. To make matters worse, they decided to toy with him before executing him. While one pointed the gun, the other beat him with a metal pipe. It looked like the end for Boris, but then two gunshots pierced the night. The Ukrainian's friends dropped dead to the ground. Like a guardian angel, Victor emerged out of the shadows, gun in hand. "Let's go," was all he said as he helped Boris up. Victor supported him as they ran away from the scene. Victor never brought up the incident again, nor did he brag about it when they were with others. Boris had trusted him completely ever since.

The two men returned to the waiting Lada. Boris said to Anna, "Well, I found Peter's car. He's at some farmhouse. I didn't see him, but there were no other vehicles in sight, so he might be there alone. He could be waiting for others." Boris paused, wondering if Anna might want to say something. She didn't. "I think we should wait until dark and if no one shows up, we can move in. Otherwise someone might walk in on us while we're trying to do the job."

"That's fine," Anna said. "But I don't want to wait too long and miss the opportunity. The moment we have a chance to finish this and leave, we should take it."

The men nodded their heads and made themselves comfortable in their seats, settling in for a stakeout. They watched village life move around them. As the sun began to set, the bazaar emptied out, and the vendors loaded their vehicles with the bread, vegetables, and other goods they had been unable to sell. Everyone seemed to have bad dental hygiene in these rural areas, Anna thought, noticing the many gold-capped teeth. Even the prettiest girl could appear sinister when smiling.

Children spilled out of homes to play in the streets as old men and mothers watched from doorways. But everyone disappeared once it became completely dark. The single lamppost by the path to the farmhouse cast a dim yellow light.

"Well, now might be the time," Boris said. The men filled their pockets with extra magazines. Anna pulled her pistol out of her purse and tucked it under the rear waist of her snug pants, pulling her expensive cashmere sweater over the weapon. Boris watched her from the corner of his eye, nervous about her participation. If anything happened to her, he would have a lot to answer for once he returned to New York City.

As they made their final preparations, a dark jeep with three men in it turned onto the street. The driver glanced at their vehicle, and they noticed a dark mark around his left temple. The jeep continued down the road and parked just past the entrance to the path that led to the farmhouse where Peter was waiting.

"Shit," Victor said, slamming his hand against the steering wheel. They watched three men exit the vehicle and, to their surprise, noticed what appeared to be assault rifles in their hands. "I wonder what's going on."

"We need to stay here. Either these men are with Peter, in which case we will be outnumbered, or they are going to kill Peter, in which case our problems will be solved," Anna said.

So they waited, growing more anxious by the minute. An hour went by and they had begun to assume the men were friends of Ivanov's, but then muffled gunfire suddenly erupted. It was faint, but there was no doubt about the sound. Boris and Victor looked at each other and then at Anna, confused. "We need to move. Whoever comes out will spot us, or the villagers will think we did it." Anna said nervously.

"Good idea," said Victor and quickly turned on the ignition. But as he did so, Peter's silver Nexia zoomed backward onto the road and then did a quick turn so that it was facing the three New Yorkers. Boris stared at the vehicle facing them as if in a standoff. The Nexia accelerated quickly toward them. "Get down!" he yelled. All three heads ducked out of view, but, as the Nexia approached, Anna peered over the dashboard. She saw two of the three men who had been in the jeep, including the man with the dark birthmark. The windshield of the Nexia was shattered, and one side of the car was riddled with bullet holes. The vehicle sped past them and onto the main street, disappearing out of sight.

"Peter wasn't inside," she said, breathing hard. "And the vehicle looked shot up."

"Maybe the men stole it. It's still quiet, so we need to figure out what happened and then get out of here before the neighbors call the police," Boris said, sitting up. They were all breathing heavily.

"Okay, let's go," Anna said, opening the door to their car and stepping out.

They walked down the road, staying to the sides, in the shadows. They saw a few lights flicker on in windows that faced the road. When they reached the entrance to the path, they walked into the trees and listened. Nothing. The three moved closer to the farmhouse, and in the darkness they made out the shapes of bodies lying on the path. Weapons ready, they continued farther down the path and looked around. They discovered four bloodied bodies, three of whom they hadn't seen before. "Two of them were just kids," Victor whispered.

"We need to search the farmhouse," Boris said quietly, and gestured to Victor to follow him. Anna waited outside. As she stared down at the lifeless face of one of the boys, she began to shake. Once the men walked into the darkness of the farmhouse, she moved toward the tree line and began retching. She thought back to how simple she had envisioned this job being while she was still in New York. Now she was standing in some remote village in Uzbekistan with dead bodies around her.

White-faced, she returned to the path and waited, looking into the trees for a possible ambush. Boris and Victor soon emerged from the dark farmhouse, their weapons no longer readied but down by their sides. Maybe Peter was dead, and they could leave this damn country, Anna silently hoped.

"No sign of Peter, or anyone else," Boris said. "The only way he could have left is through the fields in the back. If we don't follow him, we risk losing him." Boris hesitated, looking at a trembling and white-faced Anna. "Maybe you can go back to the vehicle and meet up with us farther south along the road we came in on."

"Hey Boris," Victor said quietly. "Do you ever wonder how different things would have been if you hadn't killed Peter's parents?"

Boris flashed Victor a warning look.

Anna's brow's furrowed. "Boris, is this true?"

He sighed in resignation. "Yes, it is."

"When did this happen?"

"It was a very long time ago. Almost twenty years. Around the time your mother died."

"Why did you kill them?"

After a long pause, he said, "You should ask your father."

This new revelation explained a lot, Anna thought. She simply nodded, turned around, and began walking back toward the car. She looked over her shoulder at the men. "Keep your phones on, and keep me informed," she mumbled and continued past the bodies and towards the main road.

"Yes ma'am," Boris said. The two men looked at each other and then returned to the farmhouse. At the rear, by the topchan, they stared out into the dark fields. "We need to split up. Spread out a little. We can cover more ground that way," he said while apprehensively scanning the emptiness in front of him.

"Okay, Boris. Good luck," Victor said, extending his hand to his friend. They shook hands and walked in separate directions into the darkness.

Peter walked hurriedly through fields and empty plains in the dead of night for a very long hour, trying to put as much distance as possible between himself and the farmhouse he had abandoned. To calm his nerves, he smoked the remainder of his cigarettes. He moved through open terrain, parallel to the main road running south toward Termez. He could see the distant lights of vehicles and isolated farmhouses that broke the blackness of night. Tired and dazed, he focused only on putting one foot in front of the other, often stumbling over rocks and bushes invisible in the dark. Eventually, he lay down on the grassy terrain to rest for a moment. Staring up at the brilliant array of stars that littered the sky had a calming effect on him. Thoughts of suicide diminished to a dull sense of hopelessness. He considered the value of his life and concluded that it was very low, no different from that of the dying kid he had walked away from back at the farmhouse. He thought about Madina and her bright smile and wondered what she was doing. If she truly knew the kind of person he was, she would consider him a monster and would never want to see him. He would change who he was for her. He realized that this was a pathetic, desperate notion, but his brief time with her seemed to be the only positive moment in a very long stretch of unfortunate events. The previous afternoon, when she snatched his cell phone and punched in her numbers, had been one of the brightest instants in his life. He replayed in his mind how she smiled as she turned around and walked into the restaurant. He desperately wanted to call her, but decided against it, afraid that she would notice the stress in his voice.

Having no one else to turn to, he called Alisher. No answer. He tried again, with the same result. Why? Alisher knew a call from Peter meant that he had encountered unforeseen difficulties. He needed his friend to know the truth about what had happened before he began second-guessing Peter's integrity. Escape had been his first priority, but now he needed time to think and someone to talk to.

He felt as if he could lie on the open grass forever with the stars above him, but instead he got up and began walking again, continuing to stay about a hundred yards off the main road. Thirsty, hungry, and tired, he was relieved to spot an open store along the side of the road ahead of him. Three men were sitting on crates outside the doorway, the yellow light from inside spilling onto their faces. They were old and poor, dressed in quilted blue robes with dark skullcaps. As Peter dusted off his clothes and approached the doorway, he saw that they were drinking tea and playing dominos on a small stool. They stopped speaking and looked up as Peter approached.

"Good evening," Peter said, using his best Russian in an attempt to pass as a local. "I'm looking for a place to sleep. Do you know of a room or hotel available nearby?"

The men were quiet at first, and then they spoke to each other in Uzbek, at one point seeming to argue with one another. Finally, the oldest man turned to Peter and spoke in broken Russian. "There isn't a hotel for miles. How long do you need a room for?"

"Only until the morning. I have money."

The men chatted among themselves again. The same man spoke. "We have a room in the back. I sleep there when the store is closed, but we are planning on being out here all night. It's yours for fifteen thousand *soum*."

"Throw in some food and water. and it's a deal."

"Okay," the old man said, smiling, flashing yellow-stained teeth. He got up and shuffled into the store. Peter followed him in. It was a convenience store with a variety of goods scattered among the half-filled shelves. The old Uzbek picked out a large bottle of water, a loaf of naan, and some small pieces of cheese and salami from the shelves. He led Peter through a curtained doorway. The back room was used for storage and had boxes and crates packed along the walls, with one bare lightbulb hanging loosely from the ceiling. There was one flimsy metal door secured by a padlock to the rear. Behind a wall of crates that was used as a divider, Peter found three thick blankets layered on top of each other. They looked filthy but acceptable, given the circumstances. The old man handed Peter the food and water and asked, "Where is your car, sir?"

"I don't have one. I caught a ride with some friends and was dropped off down the road," Peter said nervously. The man simply nodded his head and shuffled back out through the curtain.

Peter hungrily consumed every last bite of the bread, salami, and cheese. He then lay back on the multicolored blankets, exhausted. He felt as if he had not slept in days. He closed his eyes, thinking that the last twenty-four hours had seemed like an eternity, and drifted off before finishing that thought.

It was Boris who first spotted Peter, not too far ahead of him. Peter's large frame could barely be discerned in the darkness, but the moonlight was enough to give away his profile in the wide, open, rolling green fields. Finding him had been difficult, but Boris had pressed on without stopping or resting because he feared losing his prey. He called Anna and Victor to give his position. Only after Peter approached a small, deserted road stop did Victor catch up to Boris. Anna, with their Lada, was parked and waiting somewhere along the road. They watched Peter disappear into the café with an old man. They waited, lying on the ground for an hour after the old man emerged to join his friends, but Peter never came out. The horizon to the east was turning a light gray. It would be morning soon.

"This might be our only opportunity," Boris whispered to Victor, lying prone beside him. He called Anna and passed the news to her.

"Okay. Just finish this," was all she said before hanging up.

Victor said a short prayer, and he and Boris got up and casually walked toward the group of men who were chatting quietly in front of the café. The place was like an island of light in the dark countryside with nothing but a few sparse trees around it. "Good evening, gentlemen. We are looking for a friend of ours," Boris said, smiling disarmingly. "He's a big man in a leather jacket."

"Ah, yes. He's sleeping inside," the oldest man said. He then hesitated before asking, "Should I wake him?"

Boris looked around, seeing no one else. "No, thank you. You've already been more than helpful." He and Victor quickly drew their weapons and executed the three men, firing multiple rounds into their chests. The men never had a chance to react. They simply fell backward onto the ground, spilling domino pieces around them. The night was once again quiet, but the echo of their gunshots could be heard carrying through the countryside.

"I'll go around to the back. If Peter was sleeping, he should be awake now," Victor said and jogged to the rear of the café. Boris nodded and walked through the front door, his pistol ready in front of him.

Chapter Sixteen

Peter was awakened from his sleep for the second time this evening. He was certain the gunshots he had heard were not part of a dream. The room was dark. At first he was disoriented, wondering where he was. Once he remembered, he listened for the sounds of the old men playing and chatting outside. Hearing nothing, he slipped his jacket on and fumbled for his Makarov pistol. He looked around the crates toward the doorway, through which light spilled from the store front. If the local militia officers had connected him to last night's gunfight, the odds were against his shooting his way out. Maybe it was the men who had hijacked his heroin. Either way, he was cornered.

He saw the shadow of a pistol followed by an arm and then a large figure approach the doorway. Adrenaline rushed through his veins, and he forced himself to clear his head and focus. Peter pointed his Makarov at head level, using the crates and the darkness as cover. He decided to kill whoever came through the doorway. He had no other choice. He had no intention of going back to jail, and at this point he had nothing to lose. He had lost everything already. The shadow at the doorway hesitated for a moment and then quickly stepped into the room, ready to shoot. Peter fired three shots in quick succession at the armed man in the red track suit, the first shot hitting the target directly in the face. The man's eyes opened wide in shock, and then he crumpled to the floor, leaving the wall behind him crimson with blood.

Peter stood up slowly with his weapon still ready, waiting behind the crates for the next attacker. He took a few glances at the body lying at the foot of the doorway. It was a large Caucasian man with red hair styled into a mullet. He looked familiar, like a ghost from Peter's past. It couldn't be, he thought. "Boris?"

Hearing nothing from outside, Peter stepped around the crates and knelt next to the body, fumbling through the man's pockets with his free hand. He found an American passport and quickly opened it. Peter immediately dropped it and fell back, shocked. It was Yury's man from New York City.

Peter's palms and forehead began to perspire. His past had caught up with him. There really was no escape. Peter swore into the darkness, thinking what a fool he had been to flee to the other side of the world. Sweat dripped down his face as he realized how his problems had compounded. It was bad enough that he had lost Kurbon Usmanov's heroin, but being pursued by Yury's thugs made his situation significantly more complicated.

There were two exits: the front entrance and the back, both of which were likely to be covered. Peter opted for the rear entrance, hoping to make a quick dash into the fields and away from the road. With great effort, he picked up Boris's body and held it in front of him, using it as a shield. Holding the body up with his free hand, he shot out the padlock. Through the cracks in the doorway, he could see faint traces of gray morning light. Peter pushed open the door with his gun arm and scanned the trees and the littered yard.

He was pushed back by a series of gunshots that pummeled Boris's lifeless body. Peter fell into the café's backroom and dropped his bloodied human shield. Before he fell back, he was able to make out a moving shadow nearby, along the tree line. He moved to the left side of the doorway and quickly reached out and pulled the door so it partially closed. As he did so, shots pounded the metal door, causing a loud crashing sound that vibrated through the mountains. Through the slit between the door hinges, he was able to see the shooter waiting by the tree line to his right. The figure was standing ready by a large tree, his gun pointed at the metal door separating him from Peter. Knowing that he only had one chance at this, Peter positioned the muzzle of his pistol into the slit and carefully aimed at the figure, unsure of his accuracy. He fired one shot, needing to conserve the remaining four rounds. The figure fell back with a cry. Taking advantage of the few seconds that were afforded him by his lucky shot, Peter pushed open the doorway, rolled out, and dashed into the tree line. Gunshots kicked up dirt as he dashed toward the trees, but he managed to reach cover.

From around a large tree he stole a glance toward the wounded man lying on the grass twenty yards away. Another shot rang out, and the tree bark by his head burst into pieces. He then heard a series of empty clicks indicating a spent magazine. Taking the opportunity, Peter ran toward the prone figure. As he approached the man, Peter recognized him as someone he had seen at the Soviet, but whose name he didn't know. The bleeding man was lying on his back, fumbling in his pockets for another magazine. When he caught sight of Peter, he raised his arms, wheezing from a shot lung.

"Where is my heroin?" Peter asked flatly, pointing his pistol at Victor.

A look of genuine confusion crossed Victor's pained face. "What heroin?" Victor gasped. He was frothing saliva, unable to take in air.

Interesting, Peter thought. So they weren't the ones who took the heroin. "I'm sorry brother, but I can't have you chasing me. I'm tired of running."

"No wait—" was all Victor managed to get out before he was shot in the forehead.

Peter stared at Victor's lifeless body for a moment, his mind racing and his body still tense. Murder came easily to him now. He was desperate. Having nothing, he no longer cared about the lives of those he killed. He had nothing to lose by killing Yury's men, since he had apparently been given a death sentence already. But who had his heroin? It then occurred to him that he still had the billfold of one of his original attackers. He had forgotten about it during his escape from the farmhouse.

He pulled it out and looked through it, not knowing what to expect. Fear and surprise came over him the moment he found the man's identification. *National Security Service Major Dunyor Marasulov. Yunosobad District, Tashkent.* Peter dropped the wallet as if it burned his hands, concern furrowing his brows. He certainly was not expecting that. Even during his short time in Uzbekistan, he had heard of the NSS. The NSS was the KGB's successor in Uzbekistan, responsible for responding to domestic and foreign threats, and every other issue they considered a danger to the regime of President Islom Karimov. It was the preeminent security organization in the country, and it did whatever it saw fit. And he had killed one of its officers. The gravity of the situation began to settle on Peter, but it still left him with more questions than answers.

If Victor's reaction to Peter's question had been genuine, there was no connection between his debt to Yury and the heroin seizure by the NSS. Was the attack at the farmhouse a legitimate NSS counternarcotics operation? Did they know his identity? Was he now a wanted man? Had someone tipped them off? Was there a leak in Kurbon's organization? He wondered whether his new friend Alisher had betrayed him.

Peter quickly searched the rear of the café and the backyard littered with scrap metal and junk. He then walked into the store and looked through the front door. As he expected, the three old men he had greeted only hours before were now crumpled together on the ground. There didn't seem to be anyone else around who posed a danger. Peter knew that he did not have much time to get away. He returned to Victor's body and tossed his Makarov onto it. He looked at the corpse for a moment, wondering if the man had expected to die in a dusty hole in Central Asia. This would have been his own fate one day, Peter thought, had he also worked for Yury. He kept only his passport and money, wanting no connection to the two crime scenes he had been a part of within the last few hours.

Peter walked back through the store, controlling the panic that fought to take over. He grabbed a small bottle of vodka off the shelf and left the café, heading straight to the road. The sun's morning light was breaking over the horizon and starting to warm the night's crisp air. He poured a little of the vodka onto his chest before taking a long gulp. Once he reached the road, he began walking north, toward the bazaar in Uzun, and in the direction of Tashkent. There was very light traffic, and the security services did not seem to have been notified yet of the gunshots. He had only awoken approximately fifteen minutes ago, Peter realized. If he managed to walk away unharmed from all of this, it would be a miracle.

Once he was a sufficient distance away from the road stop, he stuck his hand out to flag a vehicle. Four passed by, but the fifth vehicle, a tiny four-door hatchback known as a Tico, came to a stop. There were three men in the car. The passenger window rolled down.

"You're drunk!" exclaimed the young man in the passenger seat, sniffing Peter and looking disgusted. "Where do you need to go? We are headed to Tashkent, but first to Samarqand."

"That sounds perfect," Peter slurred, feigning inebriation.

"Wait a minute," said the stubbled, middle-aged driver, in poor Russian. "It's going to cost you, extra even, because you will be stinking up my car. Also, we only have a rear window seat available, and the going rate is thirty thousand *soum,* but for you it will be forty thousand."

"Fine," was all Peter said before opening the flimsy car door and getting in. He wasn't about to haggle over the equivalent of forty dollars for an eight-hour car ride, especially when he desperately needed to get away. The driver beamed. The car puttered to a start and pulled back onto the dusty road.

"I would have taken you for twenty thousand!" he turned around and said to Peter, smiling mischievously.

"I would have paid one hundred thousand," Peter mumbled, closing his eyes and leaning back. The driver's smile disappeared, and the other two passengers broke out into hysterical laughter. Peter took another long gulp from the vodka bottle, feeling the warmth course through his body. He passed the bottle to the fat man next to him, who took it and drank with satisfaction. The bottle was slowly passed around to everyone, including the driver. The alcohol beginning to take effect, Peter slowly faded out of consciousness to the low rumble of the engine as the car began the long trek north.

Anna watched from a distance, in her car, as Boris and Victor's attack unfolded. She tensed when they shot the three old men outside the convenience store. She continued to hear gunshots over the next few minutes, wondering how many were needed to kill Peter. She expected Boris to emerge from the store almost immediately, but he did not. Worse, the gunshots continued, finally ending with a single shot. Sitting upright in her car, ready to pull up the vehicle to pick up the men before making a quick getaway, she could not understand what was taking so long. She did not want to call them, afraid it would distract them at a critical moment. Then, to her astonishment and horror, Peter emerged through the store's doorway alone. She called Boris's cell phone. No answer. She then called Victor. Nothing. She did not need to get out of the car and search the store to know what had happened.

Gripping the steering wheel, Anna began to shake. Since she left New York City, the situation had spiraled out of control, worsening with each passing moment, leaving more bodies in its wake. She was now alone, thousands of miles away from home, in an operation that was way over her head. Anger over her failure, grief over the likely deaths of Boris and Victor, and a creeping fear about being alone consumed her all at once, and tears streamed down her face. She watched Peter walk away down the road like an indestructible apparition, wondering what she should do now. The cost of recovering the fifty thousand Peter owed or killing him outright was increasing exponentially. Her hair was damp with sweat. She felt herself losing control, and she wondered what she had gotten herself into. Pounding the dashboard with her fists, she willed herself not to fall apart. In the midst of crying, she laughed. She laughed hysterically. She wondered if she was going mad. What was she doing in Uzbekistan? She was amazed at the fervor with which she was pursuing Peter. She found it incredible that she had set out across the planet to hunt and kill him. What had she thought would happen? She had been so foolish. Why was she doing this? Looking deeply into herself, she could not find an answer. Anna now knew that finishing Peter Ivanov would be a difficult challenge, and one that she might not survive. If Boris and Victor, with considerably more expertise, had been unable to kill him, working together, she did not think she had a good chance on her own. She struggled to reign in her emotions and think. If she could manage to finish this job successfully, then everything would be all right. She had to find a way. She stared at Peter's back as he walked away, down the road. She watched him put his hand out to hitch a ride and eventually get into a small car. Looking one last time at the deserted road stop, she pulled her Lada onto the road and followed him with newfound determination. Maybe there was still a chance she would be successful before this day was over.

Peter's quiet ride back to Tashkent was interrupted before the small Tico got very far. As they drove through Uzun, Peter noticed a heavy police presence at the street bazaar. Green uniformed militia officers were questioning shoppers and residents, and a few young men were kneeling along the side of the road with their arms folded behind their heads. A stern-faced militia officer was standing over them. *Poor fellows,* Peter thought. The young men were likely rounded up as possible suspects, but only Peter was certain of their innocence, none of them fitting the profile of the two attackers who had escaped in his car.

"I wonder what happened," mused the younger man in the passenger seat. He was rubbernecking the entire stretch of road through the town of Uzun.

"I know what happened," said the heavy-set man with wide cheeks sitting next to Peter. "Those kids were probably caught handing out harmless pamphlets on Islam and were rounded up for 'spreading extremist ideas.'"

"I doubt it," said the driver, looking grim-faced. "They were probably protesting the local government closing their shops for 'not having the proper licenses.' This happened to my cousin in Termez. Some wealthy businessman with strong connections bribed the mayor to shut down a local market so that he could build a shopping mall. The mayor told all the sellers at the market that they needed to pay an exorbitant rental fee or leave the area. What was my cousin to do? Selling fish at the market was his livelihood, and he couldn't afford the rent the mayor asked him to pay. He now has to drive sixty miles to an out-of-the-way bazaar to sell his fish. All the other sellers had to go elsewhere as well. It's a real tragedy. For what? A shopping mall that no one can afford to go to!"

Peter watched the commotion along the street but kept his face away from the window, hoping no one would recognize him. Listening to the men around him, he wondered how these Uzbeks were able to put up with a political system like this. Maybe it was because people were generally submissive by nature, going along with things until they died of old age, expecting a gentler afterlife. Everyone was frightened, and, having lived under

Soviet domination, they simply wanted to spend their days in peace without the government looking over their shoulders and interfering in their lives. Peter wondered how much misery these people could bear.

When the vehicle reached the northern border of the Surhandarya province, they found the road blocked by the militia. Every vehicle was being inspected, and there were armed officers standing by. Peter was nervous about what might happen, and he was glad that he had dumped his weapon and the NSS officer's bifold before returning north. He had remained quiet during the car ride, so he pretended to sleep as the Tico queued up to approach the barrier.

The driver shut off the engine and rolled down his window. "Good morning."

"Passport, please. Where are you headed?"

"Samarqand, and then Tashkent," the driver said, flipping his visor down to reveal his vehicle registration and passport rubber-banded to the visor. He pulled them out and handed them to the officer in green.

"Why?"

"My brother lives in Tashkent with my mother. I'm going to visit. We're stopping in Samarqand to see the Registan."

"Who are the others in your car?"

There was a silence as the driver hesitated, hoping the other passengers would now pipe up. The young man in the passenger seat leaned toward the driver's window and said, "I live in Tashkent.

I go to the Pedagogical Institute in Yakkasaroy District. I was in Termez visiting my family." He then made a motion to hand the officer his passport. But the officer gestured to another officer to go to the passenger side to inspect the student's passport. A burlier-looking man sauntered toward the passenger side, and the young man rolled down his window and gave his passport to that officer.

A quiet minute passed by as the officers looked through the passports of the driver and the student. Peter hoped this would be enough, but then he heard a tap on the glass next to his head. He opened his eyes to see the burly officer staring at him from the other side of the window, his baton ready to tap the glass again. Peter looked around groggily in feigned confusion. "Passport," the officer said impatiently.

Peter fished his passport out of his jeans pocket and handed it to the officer, looking him in the eye. "Ah, an American," said the officer, smiling. The other three in the car tensed up, surprised to find there had been an American in their car. "What is your business here in Uzbekistan?"

Peter decided to stick with the story with which he'd left Tashkent. "I am doing some work here. I went to Termez to visit a building site and to deliver some equipment," he said straight-faced, in an even voice.

"Where are your work papers?"

"What work papers?" Peter asked, remembering the paperwork sitting in the glove compartment of his Nexia. The Nexia he no longer had.

The officer grimaced, opened Peter's door, and said, "Can you step out of the car, please?"

Damn it, Peter thought, his brow beginning to sweat. He stepped out into the cool morning air. He looked around. The other officers at the checkpoint were lounging around or inspecting passports. Behind him, there was a short line of cars waiting to pass inspection and be on their way.

"Now, here in Uzbekistan, you need papers to work, especially to travel to the Surhandarya province. Are you telling me that you don't have any papers?"

Peter pretended to search through his pockets with frustration. "I had papers, but I must have left them at the building site," he said finally, looking upset and guilty.

The heavy-set officer had hairy arms and a flabby gut. He was disheveled, and he had some stubble. He was older than most of the officers, but he appeared to have the same rank. Peter thought him to be a man who cared little for how he looked and who never put a great deal of effort into anything in life. The man had probably been passed over for promotions and had worked various border checkpoints his entire career. "Well, that's not very good for you," the officer said, faint traces of a smile moving across his face.

"I promise I'll have the papers next time," Peter said quietly, pulling out a thick wad of thousand-*soum* notes from his back pocket, shielding the money so that the other officers nearby wouldn't notice. The militia officer's eyes widened at the amount. It was about a hundred dollars' worth, equivalent to a month's salary for him. Peter put the money in his palm and extended his hand in a handshake. The man looked at Peter, and his eyes narrowed. *Take the damn money,* Peter demanded silently, his heart racing. The slovenly officer glanced around and then shook Peter's hand, taking the money and slipping it into his pocket. "So is everything okay?" Peter asked, forcing a smile.

"Everything is just fine," the man said, tipping his short cylindrical cap at Peter and giving the officer on the opposite side of the Tico a thumbs-up. The officer who had first approached the driver was now inspecting the passport of Peter's companion in the back seat. He returned the passport and walked toward the next waiting vehicle. Peter decided that the heightened security wasn't in place to locate him specifically, but rather the perpetrators of last night's violent crime. Otherwise, the bribe to the militia officer would not have worked, and they would have arrested him on the spot once they saw his American passport. Peter had expected the NSS to know his identity, since they were apparently aware of the drugs changing hands at the farmhouse. Now he wasn't so sure. Either they knew but hadn't reported him to the border police, or they had no idea he had been involved.

Peter sighed in relief and opened the door to the small Tico to join his Uzbek companions. As he did so, he glanced behind him. About three cars back was a black vehicle with an attractive brunette in the driver's seat. Where had he seen that vehicle and driver before? Wasn't the vehicle a short distance from the road stop he had slipped away from at dawn? He couldn't be certain. He got into the car and closed the door.

"An American, huh?" the fat man next to him asked unemotionally.

"Yeah."

"Welcome to Uzbekistan!" the man said and extended his hand with a bright smile on his face. Peter shook it, smiling.

"Welcome!" both the driver and young man in the passenger seat said. "America is great!" the driver exclaimed in English. He then fished out an audio cassette from the clutter of wires protruding from under the dashboard and threw it into the cassette player. *Hotel California* by the Eagles came on, and he turned up the volume. He turned around, winked at Peter, and stepped on the gas, continuing on to Samarqand.

Yury Popov sat alone in his little underground office in the basement of the Soviet. He was sitting at his desk, with one hand wrapped around a small crystal glass and the other covering his eyes. On his table was a half-empty bottle of Stolichnaya vodka. Outside the heavy metal door he could hear the muffled sound of men laughing and yelling as they gambled their money away into Yury's pockets. His office was small and cramped. His table and chair took up most of the space, but the walls were lined with bookshelves that overflowed with Soviet-era memorabilia he had collected through the years. There were no chairs in front of his desk. He kept his meetings and visits short by forcing people to stand through them. He didn't want visitors getting too comfortable in his office. There was a chair to his right that his daughter usually sat in. Anna didn't like standing with everyone else, so she had brought in a chair on her own, against his wishes.

He removed his hand from his eyes and poured himself another small glass of vodka. Yury tilted his head back, poured the contents of the glass down his throat, and once again resumed his position with his hand over his eyes. He tried to control the mixture of anger, guilt, and concern that was boiling over inside him, but had a difficult time doing so. Blood continued to rush into his head, giving him a throbbing headache. Leaning back in his chair, he let out a deep breath and stared out into empty space with watery eyes.

Boris and Victor, who had always been available via cell phone, were not answering their phones. He had called Anna's hotel three times over a twenty-four-hour period but had not received a single return call. Yury wished his daughter would contact him. Peter Ivanov no longer mattered. He never really mattered that much. Finding him was not supposed to be a major undertaking. The job should have been abandoned after Peter fled to the other side of the world. It was not worth the time or money to do any more. So why was hunting down this man so important to his daughter? Yury could not understand what was driving her.

Introducing Anna to his work had been a bad idea. He had hoped to give her the opportunity to develop some administrative skills and to redirect her from the self-destructive, reckless behavior she had adopted during her studies. But from the very beginning, Anna had insisted on being involved in every aspect of his business. She did not shy away from the work, even after discovering all the nefarious activities her father was involved in. In fact, she had embraced it; so, with great trepidation, Yury had allowed her to get more deeply involved. He admitted that he now needed Anna to handle many of the day-to-day tasks he abhorred. There were so few people he could trust, so she had become an asset to him and his organization. But this work in Uzbekistan was too much. She had taken things too far. Now he just wanted his daughter home.

Part IV: Revenge

Chapter Seventeen

Seven hours after leaving Surhandarya province, the little Tico entered Samarqand, one of the greatest cities in Central Asia. Because of its location at the center of the ancient Silk Road connecting China with Europe, the warlord Amir Timur, also known as Tamerlane, who once controlled an empire stretching from India to Turkey, had made Samarqand his capital in the late fourteenth century. The city had been founded around 500 BC, making it one of the oldest inhabited cities in the world. It had been conquered over the centuries by Persians, Alexander the Great, Turks, Genghis Khan, Arabs, and most recently, Russians. Like a tour guide, the driver spoke at length about this history as his passengers listened and took in their surroundings.

Samarqand's history was not at first apparent to Peter as the vehicle moved through the streets, since many of the shops and buildings appeared contemporary by Central Asian standards, though Peter did notice historic structures like the Bibi-Khanym Mosque and the Guri Amir Mausoleum, situated like islands in a sea of modernity. The streets were crowded with pedestrians and vehicles, leaving no doubt that Samarqand was the second largest city in Uzbekistan.

The Tico finally came to a stop in front of the Registan, the most impressive set of structures Peter had ever seen. The Registan was comprised of three massive madrasas, their imposing rectangular portals surrounding the large square in the middle. Public executions had been held in the square until the early twentieth century. Two of the madrasas were flanked on each side by tall minarets. They were all covered with detailed mosaics that gleamed in the midday sun. These madrasas were the center of Islamic theology in the fifteenth-century Muslim world, the golden age of Samarqand. Later, the city became a commercial center where caravans from all over Asia would come to trade.

The three Uzbeks got out of the car and walked to a large platform that looked out over Registan's square. Peter exited the car and followed them at a distance, groggy from the nap he had taken during the seven-hour car ride. Not waiting for Peter, the Uzbeks walked down a wide flight of stairs that led to the square. When Peter reached the platform, he looked at his travel companions standing in the square below among the massive madrasas. They were like ants in relation to the ancient structures, even though the Uzbeks were only a little more than one hundred meters away from him. The scene was certainly panoramic, and he was thankful they had chosen this detour.

"It's impressive, isn't it?" a female voice asked from behind him in clear American English. Peter spun around, and he saw the woman he had spotted in the dark sedan at the checkpoint many hours ago. He also realized that he had seen her before: she was Yury's daughter, Anna. He tensed immediately. He looked around for more of Yury's goons but saw none.

She moved to the railing alongside him, but stayed an arm's length away. Looking closely at her face, Peter saw that she was tired. Her eyes were bloodshot, her mascara was a little smudged, and her hair was slightly unkempt. On a normal day, he would have thought her beautiful, but today her face was pale and gaunt. "You're a difficult man to find, Mr. Ivanov." Her cracked lips forced a smile. "You've picked a hell of a place to escape to."

She didn't appear to be armed, but Peter wasn't sure. "You shouldn't have come here," he said tensely.

"Tell me, Peter. Do you remember the first time we met?"

"What are you talking about?"

"The first time you and I ever met. Do you remember?"

Peter had no idea what she was getting at. He didn't remember ever meeting her. He had just seen her around the Soviet during his last month in Brighton Beach. That was all. "Is this a trick question? We've never met before."

She looked at him for a silent moment with an unreadable expression. He wondered what this was all about. Her face changed, and she switched topics.

"You shouldn't have run. Do you always flee from your responsibilities?" she asked with a smirk. "Are you a coward?"

"Your father gave me no choice."

She looked at him curiously. "It was your choice to throw away your money at our establishment, and then you borrowed some more. You knew exactly what you were doing."

He knew that she was right. Maybe he was a coward. "I'm sorry, Ms. Popova, but I can't pay you. You should go back to New York." He looked fiercely at her. "Just leave me alone."

Her face became hard. "Whatever scheme you have going to get rich will not redeem you from the menace you have become to my father and me." She took a step closer to him. "Enjoy these moments and days while you have them, Mr. Ivanov, because you will not leave this country alive. I will make sure of it."

Peter didn't like being threatened. He also took a step toward her, putting his face a foot away from hers. "You haven't had much luck killing me so far."

She looked at him contemptuously. "You think you're really something," she said, sneering and shaking her head. "You're a nobody, Peter. You are nothing to this world."

Looking into her eyes, Peter saw that she believed what she said. It wasn't an empty put-down. She turned around and walked away, back to the street behind him. He didn't watch her go. He looked straight ahead at the magnificent view in front of him. The sun shone brightly on his face, so he closed his eyes. He knew that this world didn't want him. Nevertheless, he promised himself that he wouldn't go without a fight.

Madina woke up feeling despondent and knew it was going to be a bad day. She didn't know if she was upset about her life or her work. Her work was both a blessing and a curse. She loved the attention, the way men looked at her admiringly, the way women looked at her with jealousy, and the money she made from the tips wealthy patrons threw onto the dance floor. Unfortunately, she needed to put up with a lot of abuse in order to hold on to one of the most coveted dancing roles in Tashkent. She was admired by some of the wealthiest and most influential men in the city. But these men, as valued patrons, were able treat the dancers as their own personal harems. They wanted to meet the girls, take them out, sleep with them, or marry them. The owner urged the girls to be friendly and did not discourage fraternizing with wealthy customers if it meant repeat business. Many of the girls played along in order to keep their jobs, never mentioning how far they had taken things. A few were in fact happy, because it meant the opportunity to live better, more comfortable lives than the ones they had. But being dumped after sleeping with a patron was a common complaint.

Madina wanted no part of it, but the atmosphere was starting to affect her work. Even though she continued to perform well, the fact that she rebuffed her admirers upset restaurant management, and they threatened to replace her unless she became friendlier. As the star dancer of the show, she had some leverage, but not enough. She wasn't entirely opposed to dating these men. No doubt a few of them were good catches. However, most of them were crooked, and their wealth was tied to staying in Uzbekistan. Sure, they had foreign accounts, but they had dedicated their lives to serving and enriching their political leaders, whom they could not abandon. For this reason, Madina was even more determined to find a way out of her current dilemma, and, more important, out of Uzbekistan.

When she considered her options, Peter came to mind. There was something about him that intrigued her. Behind his smile and charm, she sensed loneliness and fear. He seemed sure of himself and even arrogant, but Madina was certain it was a facade. He also seemed humble about his work, which was unusual among Bahor's regular patrons. She decided that if he called, she would go out with him. One date couldn't hurt.

Peter was back in Tashkent by early evening. He was tired but happy to be in a big city again, where he could easily blend in or disappear altogether. He felt most at home in urban environments, whether it was New York City, Sarajevo, or Tashkent. The teeming crowds and bright lights invigorated his tired mind and aching body. Being in the midst of the hubbub of city life made him feel as if he was part of something bigger. When he was along the Uzbek-Tajik border, walking through the hills in the middle of the night with no one around him, he felt alone and feared that he might never see the civilized world again. For some reason, he feared dying in the middle of nowhere more than dying in a city.

Peter thought an urban death, no matter how tragic or violent, would at least be noticed or memorialized. He had a good idea of what would happen in the dark depths of Uzbekistan's border areas. His body would be stripped and thrown in a ditch, never to be seen again. No one would ever know who he was. He would rest forever in some unmarked grave. He recalled the family of traffickers he had seen murdered and regretted leaving that poor boy to die alone in the dark. It was a meaningless end to an insignificant life, and Peter hoped he would be spared the same fate. He shook these morbid thoughts out of his mind. He never knew why his thoughts always drifted in this direction.

Not wanting to highlight his final destination, Peter bid his fellow travelers good-bye and exited the small Tico in front of the Drujba Narodova concert hall. He immediately walked down a set of stairs leading underground into the subway station. The subway system in Uzbekistan had four lines and could take a traveler to the general vicinity of most districts. Because Tashkent was the Soviet base from which all of Central Asia was governed, the city enjoyed prestigious universities and cultural centers, in addition to having the only subway system in the region. Each station was artistically designed according to the theme or person the station was commemorating. The trains ran on time, were very clean, and a traveler could ride from any station to another for the equivalent of a quarter.

Peter used the subway system to get off the surface roads, hoping to throw Anna off his trail. He had occasionally checked for her black Lada during the last hours of the drive from Samarqand to Tashkent. She was always there, staying behind the

Tico at a discreet distance. He knew that another confrontation with her was inevitable, but he wanted to do it at his own time and place of choosing.

Foremost on his mind was getting some answers. He had to clear his name with Alisher and Kurbon, who most likely suspected him of betrayal. He had been passively reacting to events around him, placing most of the control and decision-making in the hands of others. That needed to change.

At the bottom of the stairs, Peter walked through a set of glass doors and entered the station. He purchased a blue plastic token from a uniformed woman, inserted the coin into a turnstile, and walked down a set of marble stairs toward the platform. The waiting hall was cavernous and elegant, with a high, rounded ceiling holding glass chandeliers, and a wide and very long platform with islands of stone benches running through the middle. There were many locals standing along either side, waiting for a train to arrive. Digital counters above each tunnel indicated how many minutes had passed since the last train had departed, giving the waiting passengers an approximate idea of how much longer they would have to wait. Typically a train ran every eight minutes. There were also militia officers standing on the platforms, keeping their eyes out for travelers who appeared suspicious. They casually paced back and forth, not completely alert, half-distracted by attractive girls. Peter avoided eye contact and faced away from them toward the tunnel, hoping that he wouldn't be noticed. He thought he blended in with the few ethnic Russians also waiting for the train, but he still smelled of alcohol and looked exhausted. Besides, he didn't know if a bulletin had gone out with his description or name. He noticed out of the corner of his eye that an officer was walking past, and Peter felt the Uzbek's eyes on his back, but the man didn't approach. A green-colored train screeched into the hall and came to a stop. Peter rushed in before the militia officer could decide whether he warranted an identification check.

Twenty minutes later, he emerged out of the Mashinasozlar subway station, and, after checking to be sure that Anna had not exited the station with him, he pulled out his cell phone and called Alisher. This time his friend picked up.

"Peter?"

"Yeah, it's me."

"I'm glad to hear from you." There was a pause. "Listen, we just got word from our friends in Kazakhstan. They never made contact with you. What the hell is going on?"

"Alisher, we need to talk," was all Peter was able to say. He did not know whether he could trust his former cellmate. For all he knew, Alisher was feigning ignorance. "We need to talk in person."

"Peter, deliver the goods and then come back. We can talk afterward. Mr. Usmanov is about to go berserk. He's ready to send everyone out to find you. And believe me, it's not to give you a bonus for good performance."

"Alisher, that's what I need to speak with you about. There's been a problem. A big problem. If you don't meet with me immediately, we're both going to face a lot of heartache from Mr. Usmanov," Peter said, emphasizing every word to make himself clear. He guessed that if Alisher had really played no part in what happened in Uzun, the fact that he had vouched for Peter was enough for the Usmanovs to seriously question Alisher's loyalty. "Can I trust you to come and meet with me alone?"

There was another pause. Peter hoped the implication of what he had said was sinking in. "When?" Alisher asked.

"Right now."

"Where?"

"Botkina Cemetery. South of Parkent Bazaar," Peter said.

"I'll be there in twenty minutes. Meet me by the memorial to the football team that perished in the plane crash." With those words, Alisher hung up.

Peter walked north from the subway station and eventually reached Habiba Abdulaeva Prospect, a major thoroughfare coming from the west and curving north. Heading north, he reached Botkina Cemetery, one of the largest cemeteries in Tashkent. There was a short path leading from the road to the cemetery gates. On either side of the path were small shops and vendors selling flower arrangements. They called out and beckoned to Peter as he walked by. Peter walked through the iron gates that marked the entrance and took in his surroundings. Botkina Cemetery was a large Soviet-era Christian burial ground, used mostly by ethnic Russians and Christian Uzbeks. From the gates, a path led straight to a small, light-blue Orthodox church. To either side of the path were rows upon rows of family burial plots crammed together, separated only by short fences and railings. The tombstones were of all shapes, colors, and sizes, uniquely designed, and all carried an image of the deceased. Usually the image was of only the face, but occasionally full portraits were etched into the stone. Passersby would always know what the deceased looked like at the age of their death. Peter sensed the eyes on the tombstones staring at him as he walked by.

Immediately to the right of the entrance was the memorial Alisher had mentioned. The graves of the football players were arranged in a circle with a small black-and-white portrait of each player facing out. The men were young and handsome, but their faces were solemn. Behind their graves was a single grave with a stone football floating above it. At the head was the picture of the older, white-haired coach. Peter remembered hearing his parents talk about an entire Soviet Republic of Uzbekistan football team perishing in an airplane crash in the late seventies on their way to a match in Russia. They were subsequently honored as heroes.

Peter wanted to avoid surprise, so he moved away from the memorial and into the rows of gravesites across the path. There, he stood between two rows of high tombstones, to screen him from the memorial to the perished team. From here, he observed the memorial. If Alisher came with company, it would confirm that he could not be trusted and prove that their friendship was artificial at best. As Peter waited, time seemed to slow, and he became anxious. The sun had just set, and the dimly lit sky shone on the hunched babushkas dressed in old coats and shawls, and the homeless in their rags, walking zombie-like through the cemetery.

Peter considered calling Alisher again, but then a lone figure walked through the entrance and to the memorial. He stood there and looked around. Yes, it was Alisher, and he appeared to be alone. Peter cautiously walked over to him, checking his surroundings along the way.

Alisher looked sharp in black dress pants, a collarless, tight black shirt, and polished black dress shoes. He was starting to look like Kurbon's spoiled nephew, Ravshan. Peter looked haggard by comparison in his dusty, white button-down shirt and blue jeans. As he approached, Alisher gave a tight, forced smile while looking him over. "You don't look very good," Alisher said.

"And you look like you're well taken care of."

"Being promoted has its perks." Then, "So why are we here?"

Peter briefly summarized the events of the previous night. "The entire plan went south after I got to Uzun. The traffickers showed up and passed the heroin to me, but as soon as it was loaded in my car, we were ambushed by three masked gunmen. The traffickers were killed on the spot before the gunmen took off in my Nexia, but I managed to take one of them out. I checked the body's ID and it turned out to be an NSS officer from Yunosobad here in Tashkent. Anyway, I fled the scene and managed to hitch a ride back here," Peter said, studying his friend, waiting for a reaction. Alisher was stone-faced.

"So the drugs are gone," his former cellmate muttered, looking down. It was a statement, not a question. "And the NSS is behind it."

Peter nodded. He had left out the second attack by the New

York mobsters. Alisher didn't need to know about that. Plus, it was his own business that he alone had to take care of. No reason to complicate the story. "Anyway, you and Mr. Usmanov need to know that it wasn't me. I didn't run away with it, nor did I fence it. I was set up."

"Either way, it's a lot of money. Kurbon will go into a rage. He's going to want that heroin back, no matter what the story is. I believe you, but he will not. Your word doesn't mean a whole lot to him. We need some evidence, or at least more information about who was behind it. Maybe then you—I mean we—can present the evidence to Kurbon and tell him what happened. Otherwise, someone's head will have to roll," Alisher said with sympathy. Peter had a pretty good idea of whose head it would be. "I'm sorry, Peter."

"Well, I'm a big boy, and I knew what I was getting into. Anyway, I have an idea about how I can get more information, if not the heroin, but I'm going to need some time. I need you to cover for me for as long as possible. Can you do that for me?"

Alisher considered this for a moment. "Okay. I hope whatever you have planned is good." He hesitated and then dug into his pocket and pulled out a single key with a numbered tag. "I have a room at the Grand Orzu Hotel. It's where we spent the night after our celebratory night out. Take the room. I don't need it. This way you can stay off the grid, and the NSS, if they are searching for you, will not be tipped off to your location. You won't have to show your passport to check in."

Peter reluctantly took the key. "Thanks. I'll call you when I have something."

Alisher's cell phone rang. He looked at the caller ID but didn't take the call. Peter noted a look of uneasiness on his friend's face. "I need to go, Peter," was all he said before he walked back toward the entrance gate. Peter stood at the memorial for a moment, watching his friend as he walked away. Alisher answered his cell phone when he was by the gate and out of earshot. Peter was grateful to have a place to rest but wondered how much time he really had before Alisher stopped granting favors and began looking after his own best interests.

In the hotel room, Peter stripped down and showered. It felt like his first shower in months. The water draining at his feet was stained yellow from two days of dirt, grime, and sweat. For a long time, he stood in the tub with the water dripping down his body, staring at the gray tiles around him as his mind drifted. Starting tomorrow, he was going to take matters into his own hands. He knew that no matter what happened, his business with Kurbon, the NSS, the heroin, and Anna would be settled within the next few days. Unless he resolved all his problems, his time on earth would run out soon.

But first, he wanted to see Madina. He needed to see her. Once he was dried and dressed, he called her.

"Hello?" a soft voice said.

"It's Peter. How are you?"

"Fine, but I'm already at the restaurant. I'm going to start rehearsing soon. I'm glad you called, though."

That was a good sign. "Thank you. Listen, I'm back in Tashkent, and I was hoping to see you tonight. Are you available after work?"

"Um, yes, I am free."

"Good, I'll meet you outside your restaurant a little after 11:00 PM, after your show ends."

"Perfect," she said and hung up. Things were already starting to go his way.

After losing sight of Peter, Anna returned to the Dostlik Hotel. She was drained from the long drive back to Tashkent, saddened at having lost Victor and Boris, and frightened by the prospect of failing and returning home empty-handed. Peter had managed to evade her again. To make matters worse, the hotel receptionist had told her that a Yury Popov had called for her three times while she was away. She still hadn't informed her father about Boris's and Victor's deaths. Telling him the bad news was the last thing she wanted to do. Once in her room, she quickly drained a miniature bottle of vodka from the minibar. She hadn't changed her clothes since she left Tashkent, so she stripped off the black outfit she had worn for the last two days. Her dark, curly hair was matted with sweat, and her skin felt oily. She gave a long sigh, hating how she felt. She missed New York—roughing it in the Third World was not her definition of fun. Without thinking, she picked up a glass ashtray sitting on the coffee table and flung it against a wall, shattering it into pieces. She was shocked by this act, and her inability to control it. She stared at the dent in the wall and the broken pieces of glass scattered across the floor. *That was a stupid thing to do,* she thought. Now she had to pick up all the pieces or risk stepping on one.

Anna considered her conversation with Peter. The brief encounter in Samarqand was the first time she had stood face-to-face with him since she was fifteen. All this time she had demonized him in her mind, but, after speaking with him, she realized that he was just a desperate, vulnerable human being. A messed-up loser. She remembered the hurt look in his eyes after what she had said about the world not wanting him. Anna wondered if he was worth all the trouble she had gone through. She wondered what difference it would have made in the long run had she abandoned her search after realizing that he had fled the United States. But now it was too late. She was here in Uzbekistan, she had struck a deal with the Usmanovs, and Boris and Victor were dead. She was determined to follow through on finishing Peter.

She picked up her room phone and called Kurbon Usmanov. Even though she despised him, he was the only person who could salvage her trip to Tashkent. "Good evening, Ms. Popova," Kurbon's voice said on the other end. She thought he sounded tired.

"Hello, Mr. Usmanov. How are you?"

"Busy. How can I help you?"

She did not appreciate the question, sure that he knew exactly how he could help her. She forced her voice to remain even. "I need to meet with you. Soon, if possible."

"Well, I can't tonight. In fact, I'm busy tomorrow as well." Then, after a pause, "I can meet briefly tomorrow night. Come by the Café Three Oranges at about eight."

Anna would have preferred to have been asked. "Okay. I'll see you then." She heard his line disconnect. She slammed the receiver down in frustration.

Still naked, she walked into her bathroom, turned on the shower, and stepped in. Once the hot water began running over her body, she started crying.

Chapter Eighteen

The next morning, Kurbon Usmanov sat on his usual *topchan* under a shaded mulberry tree by the gently flowing stream. He was wearing a quilted purple robe, looking pensive while drinking green tea, staring at nothing in particular. The morning was bright and promised to be a warm day, but he had a gloomy air about him. The outdoor teahouse was devoid of customers, save his men. This was to be expected, since it was payday. His men were scattered about the clearing, talking and laughing among themselves. One at a time, the men approached a nearby *topchan* where Ravshan sat with a large duffel bag filled with files and envelopes. Ravshan dug through the bag for the proper envelope and handed it to the employee, who accepted the payment appreciatively with a short bow, his right hand flat against his chest. He walked away so the next man could approach. As they walked away from Ravshan, they made a similar gesture to the senior Usmanov, but he only responded with a nod of his head.

Kurbon was feeling reflective. He looked around him and thought about the life he had built for himself and his nephew. He remembered being young and having nothing. He remembered constantly searching for work in Termez and always being subordinate to others. His life was much better now, and he could proudly say that he had done it all himself. Even with the setbacks he had experienced, he considered himself lucky. He reminded himself that he had a lot to be thankful for. His life was comfortable, and he had more wealth than the great majority of Uzbeks, who had little hope and lived a meager existence. He had twenty men working directly for him as muscle. He owned the Café Three Oranges, and the teahouse, where he employed another thirty people as cooks, bartenders, waitresses, and managers. He made about three thousand dollars a month in profit. This was far less than what he had made before Alisher was arrested, and the trafficking business went under, but the figure still dwarfed the salaries of over 99 percent of his countrymen. He expected his income to grow exponentially with his entry into the drug trade. But this venture was poised to fall apart if Peter did not make the delivery. Kurbon kicked himself for foolishly trusting a man he did not know for such an important task. His desperation had blinded his good sense and convinced him to take a risky gamble. He wished he had sent someone along to watch the American. Now it was too late. It had taken a considerable amount of work to find and convince the Kazakh businessmen to join him in this endeavor. Kurbon did not want to disappoint his partners with a missed delivery, especially since they had paid two hundred thousand in advance. Not to mention that the Usmanov reputation would be spoiled and it would be very difficult to secure future partners. He already had enough enemies. The last thing he needed was two more.

He saw Alisher enter the clearing. Ravshan now handled the bookkeeping, but Kurbon was nevertheless happy that Alisher was back. He was reliable, trustworthy, intelligent, and had made a tremendous personal sacrifice in order to protect the Usmanovs. Even his men respected and loved Alisher. He was the best asset the Usmanovs had, and Kurbon wished his nephew appreciated that. And had some of the same virtues. He also wondered whether Alisher held any resentment or anger toward him for the prison sentence.

Kurbon nodded at Alisher as he approached the *topchan.* "Alisher, please sit down," Kurbon said and handed him a cup of green tea. They exchanged their morning pleasantries quickly, wanting to get down to business. "So, what news do you have for me?" was all the elder Usmanov asked, still looking off into the distance.

Alisher took a deep breath and spoke. "I had an unexpected but interesting meeting last night. It was with an NSS officer named Salim Guliyamov. I'm sure you remember him, because I sure do. He called me and told me that it was in my best interest to meet with him, so I reluctantly agreed to it. During this brief meeting he told me that he had the heroin. He admitted to taking it from Peter during the exchange and killing the traffickers." Alisher said all this while looking intently at Kurbon, seemingly to discern his reaction.

"The NSS?" Kurbon asked with surprise.

Alisher seemed to be choosing his words carefully, keeping his voice low so that the other men would not hear. "Salim wants a share of the profits from here on. He considers this a normal business practice, done frequently to ensure that nothing goes wrong with the authorities. If you are willing to accept this proposal, he will return the heroin. Otherwise, I think we can expect more trouble down the road."

Kurbon slammed his palm onto the small table resting in the middle of the platform, his dark skin turning a shade of red. The men standing nearby turned around, startled, and then resumed their conversations as they moved away. Alisher remained quiet. A few moments later, Kurbon said in a strained voice, "No. We are not going to let this man bleed us dry. If we give him money now, he will continue to ask for more. Plus, we are the ones taking the risks. Why should we give him a share?"

"Well, our risks would be minimized if we could ensure safe passage and avoid scrutiny by the authorities."

"How can we know that?" Kurbon asked harshly. "A problem could still arise and we would be told that we didn't pay off the right people. Eventually, border guards and NSS officers from every district will want a piece of the profits from operating in their jurisdictions. How do we know if this man is connected or will take care of us properly? We know very little about him. This officer has a lot of nerve threatening us. Threatening me!"

"And what if he is working with others? What if he is being directed to blackmail us by more powerful people?"

"It doesn't matter," Kurbon said flatly. "It changes nothing."

Alisher didn't say anything, and the two sat quietly for a moment. Kurbon leaned over to him and whispered, "This is the man who arrested you and then asked for a bribe. I paid it, but he still ruined me and imprisoned you!" Tears of anger were forming in Kurbon's eyes, and his hands shook. "I am done paying useless bribes and trying to buy our way out of trouble. This man is our enemy. I want you to find this Salim. Find him, find my drugs, and then kill him. I'm not going to let some greedy NSS officer ruin everything that I have built."

His tone softened, and he continued reassuringly, "We will grow, Alisher. We will become more powerful. We will have enough resources to save ourselves from whatever problems come up." He rested a hand on Alisher's shoulder. "You will become rich. You will get everything you want. And most important, you will have revenge." Kurbon sighed and looked away for a moment. Then, as an afterthought, he said, "Also, Peter can still be useful to us. Find him and bring him here." Kurbon paused and looked closely at Alisher, hoping he had convinced him to trust his judgment. He needed Alisher now more than ever. "Are you with me, my friend?"

"Yes. Yes, of course I'm with you. I'll take care of everything," Alisher said as he scooted off the *topchan* and onto his feet. "I'll contact you once I have a lead."

As he turned to walk away, Kurbon said in a low voice, "My son, not everything in life is supposed to be easy."

Alisher nodded, turned around, and walked out of the clearing.

That very same morning, Peter woke up feeling invigorated and upbeat as he thought about the terrific evening he had had with Madina the previous night. They had met and gone to the National Park for a late walk in the cool air. Madina was guarded at first, but her caution dissolved quickly, and she opened up. She was inquisitive and had many questions about the world outside of Uzbekistan. She asked about the United States as if it were some mythical, imaginary place. She had never been abroad, so she was fascinated by the most mundane things. She wanted to know about the shopping, the food, the movies, and many other aspects of everyday life. She wondered if people needed permission or paperwork to travel. She questioned the safety of the cities. She even asked if anyone was poor, given how rich America was as a country. Peter was proud of his ability to field all her questions and help her understand life in the United States. He had jokingly suggested taking her there one day so she could see the country firsthand, to which she laughed, played along, and said, "Okay." He recalled how beautiful she had looked with her wavy, dark hair flowing around her angel-like face, with its wide smile and full lips. Her light olive complexion had looked flawless in the moonlight. They were not together long because of the late hour. But to Peter's relief, she suggested getting together again, preferably during the day when she had more time. Afterward, he put her in a cab and returned to his hotel alone.

His muscles were sore and he wanted more rest, but he had to focus on his task for the day, which was to track down a crooked NSS officer. He only had one lead. The officer he had killed in Uzun was from the Yunusobad district of Tashkent, so Peter hoped the man whose face he saw in the jeep was from the same office. He got dressed, walked out of the Grand Orzu Hotel, and flagged a cab to the Yunosobad Bazaar located at the heart of the similarly named district.

The bazaar was packed in the early morning with haggling shoppers and traders. The open-air market was arranged in colorful rows of stalls selling fruits, vegetables, nuts, seasonings and spices, bread, honey, eggs, homemade cakes, sweets, and even vats of Korean kimchi. The cheese, chicken, beef, horse meat, and river fish were sold indoors in a building adjoining the outdoor stalls. Wine, beer, juices, and household products were also sold indoors. Peter wondered how the products stayed fresh in the blistering summers. The bazaar vendors drove into the city for the day from regions outside of Tashkent with their goods loaded into small vehicles. They were dressed in traditional clothing—the few people in the city who actually were.

Peter scanned the crowds and found the person he was looking for. He spotted a militia officer in the typical dark green uniform with a flat conical hat, similar to those worn by the men at the checkpoints he had passed through the previous day. The officer he spotted was young, clean-shaven, and wearing a crisp uniform, which meant that he was new to the job and afraid of making mistakes. Most important, he had an air of authority about him. Peter judged that the young man was proud of his role in society, and probably had not yet become cynical or jaded, or taken any bribes. He was speaking in the shade with a heavy-set man selling pomegranates. Peter walked up to him and offered his hand. The officer looked at Peter with a cautious smile but took his hand and shook it. "Pardon me, officer, but I have a question that you might be able to help me with," Peter said as he turned the officer away from the vendor so the man couldn't listen in. "I have an appointment at the Yunosobad district's NSS office, and it's very important. Do you know where it's located?"

The young officer's smile disappeared, and he looked at Peter with new interest. With raised eyebrows, he exclaimed: "I can't tell you that! Why do you need to know?"

Peter lowered his voice and said, "Sir, I report to Officer Dunyor Marasulov every month with information that is of interest to him. It's how I earn a living and how he gets good leads that get him promoted. Usually we hold our scheduled meetings on the street, but this time I have some important news for him, so he asked me to come to his office. I was so nervous I forgot to ask for directions. I hate being late because he has a terrible temper."

The man considered this for a moment, clearly suspicious of Peter. "I understand, but it's not the kind of information we give out," the officer said quietly, looking around him.

"He asked me to come to his office this morning at 10:00 AM, and it's already 9:45. Maybe you can escort me there and walk me through the door if that is more comfortable for you. You can even confirm that Officer Marasulov has an appointment with me," Peter said, attempting to appear at ease and confident. "He doesn't like it when others know who his sources are, but I'm sure he will make an exception this time since you're only being helpful."

The officer was looking anxious, having been put in a difficult situation. The NSS was the most feared government institution in the country, and crossing an NSS officer could have serious negative repercussions. He studied Peter again and said, "I'm going to have to see your passport."

This isn't good, Peter thought. He had to think fast. "Okay, here it is," he said, showing the cover of his American passport.

The officer's eyes widened a little, realizing that Peter was no street bum. "You're an American," he muttered as he reached for the passport.

Peter did not hand it over immediately. "I must tell you, you are free to inspect it, but now that I have told you why I need to go to the NSS office, I need to write down your badge number and name, because Marasulov wants the identities of everyone who knows about our clandestine relationship." With that, Peter handed over his passport. "So, if you could just write down your information—"

The officer stood frozen, staring at the passport cover while weighing the pros and cons of giving the information to this American. He then handed the passport back to Peter without looking at it. "All right. The office is on Zakirova Street, just east of the Habib Abdullaeva subway station. But don't tell anyone I told you this, especially this NSS friend of yours."

"I completely understand. Thank you, my friend." Peter shook the young man's hand and walked away, weaving toward the northern side of the bazaar and exiting through the gates. He looked behind him to confirm that the militia officer was not trailing him. Along the street were rows of idling cars, waiting to intercept shoppers who might need a taxi ride. He walked past them and turned east on a road with some vehicular traffic and no foot traffic. He walked until he found what he was looking for. He saw a white Matiz, a small four-door hatchback similar to the Tico, and common to Tashkent roads. He looked around him and didn't see anyone. Perfect.

Three minutes later, Peter was driving the Matiz south on Amir Timur Street. It had been a long time since he had hot-wired and stolen a vehicle, but it came back quickly, like riding a bike. At the Habib Abdullaeva subway station he turned left on Zakirova Street as instructed. As he drove, he thought about what he was going to do. His plan was simple. He was going to find a place to hunker down outside of the building, wait for the officer with the birthmark to exit, and then follow him to a place where he could ask the man some questions, privately.

Salim Guliyamov sat at his desk and stared at the shadows cast by the red light shining into his office from the setting sun. He was having one of those days. Marasulov's death was the least of his concerns. He had explained away Marasulov's unfortunate demise as an operation gone bad. Arrangements were already being made for his family to receive his pension. As the most senior officer at the Yunosobad branch, Salim did not worry about whether the officers he interacted with on a day-to-day basis suspected what really happened. They would never confront or question him. As far as he was concerned, the book on his subordinate's death was closed.

His anxiousness stemmed from those higher up his chain of command. His superiors knew exactly what had happened in Uzun. As a matter of fact, they had sanctioned the operation. But they wanted the remaining loose ends tied up, and, more important, they wanted the money they expected to receive from Kurbon Usmanov. It was Salim's job to convince the man that he needed to be a team player, and Alisher was the key to the plan. If Alisher was smart, there would be nothing to worry about. If only his superiors were more patient …

Salim put out the cigarette he was smoking and stifled a yawn. He finished prioritizing the paperwork that had accumulated over the past two days while he was away. As he was preparing to leave, his telephone rang. He hesitated to pick up the phone, afraid the call might tie him up for the evening. Eventually, after several rings, he picked up the receiver.

"Good afternoon."

"Salim, how are you?" The voice was familiar.

"Hello, sir. How are you? How is your family?"

"Fine. Thanks for asking. I have been trying to call you all day. Either you haven't been at your desk, or you are avoiding me."

"No sir, not at all. I was meaning to speak with you. I had a productive meeting last night with one of Usmanov's deputies. I think our problems will be resolved soon."

"Is that so? Well, I hope you're right." Then, after a pause, "Salim, if you are not up to this, I can call someone else who has the time and the commitment to our common goals."

"No sir, you don't want to do that. I'm the man you want. I can do this. Just give me some more time."

"Good. I'm glad to hear that. I like you, Salim. Your family will appreciate the rewards your hard work will bring. Call me with an update tomorrow." The line went dead.

Salim sighed, put down the receiver, and walked out of his office. He locked the door behind him and walked down the hall. Half-heartedly, he saluted good-bye to the men he saw in the hallway.

He stepped out of the three-story building and into the small parking lot adjoining it; a high steel fence separated the two. Once he was in his red Nexia, he lit another cigarette and pulled out of the secure lot and onto Zakirova Street. The roads were crowded with cars, the sidewalks with students, shoppers, workers, and vagrants. He slowly made his way home, not noticing how long it took because his thoughts were elsewhere.

Salim remembered how eleven years ago, he had worked as a secondary school chemistry teacher, an occupation that had promised good job security. The world he had known had unexpectedly collapsed, however, with the fall of the Soviet Union. The independent country of Uzbekistan came into being, and the economic rules that had governed society for so long had changed. Many sectors of the economy became more market-driven, and people like Salim wondered whether their jobs would survive this turbulent period. During this time, the Uzbekistani arm of the KGB divorced itself from Russia. It became an independent security and intelligence service, calling itself the National Security Service. A call went out for young, educated, skilled men and women to join its ranks and protect the newborn country from foreign and domestic threats. Salim had joined with the best of intentions. In fact, he was pleased by many of his and his colleagues' accomplishments. But the private sector flourished, and entrepreneurs in business began to make a lot of money. For the first time, there were large wage disparities among the working class in Uzbekistan, and those in government services suffered the most. Salim's wages became insufficient to provide for his family as prices for goods quickly rose. To compensate for his low wages, he started making small amounts of money on the side by clearing fines, brokering contacts, and shaking down criminals.

At first he had a guilty conscience, but he rationalized his actions as being necessary to survive. The extra income helped make ends meet and carried him through life for a very long time. Then, quite suddenly, six months ago, he had been diagnosed with cancer. The hospitals in Uzbekistan no longer provided the care he needed for free, as they had for citizens of the Soviet Union. His treatments were expensive and drained his savings. He needed more money, desperately. His predicament had come to the attention of his superiors. He was contacted and given an opportunity to save himself and his family from a life of poverty.

Salim's thoughts came back to the present as he approached his neighborhood in Uchtepe, a lower-class district on the western outskirts of the city. Most government employees lived in the outer districts of Tashkent because housing prices were relatively cheaper. Most people, including Salim, lived in Soviet-style apartment blocks. Addresses were given as a series of numbers: the neighborhood number, the building number, and then the apartment number.

The sun had set and it was now growing dark. Salim pulled into a vacant alley with small, gray metal garages on both sides that were all similarly shed-like in shape and design. He stopped his car in front of one and stepped out to open the padlocked door. The padlock was old, rusted, and needed some jiggering to unlock. He opened the door and stepped into the dark garage. He pulled a flashlight off the shelf by the entrance and turned it on to provide some light, illuminating the tools, boxes, and litter cluttered inside. He heard an engine rev up and approach but thought nothing of it, dismissing it as one of the many sounds that were common in the early evening hour. He set his still-lit flashlight back on the shelf and turned back toward his car.

As he approached the front of his vehicle, he saw a set of headlights coming quickly toward him without any indication that the vehicle was slowing down. He wasn't able to move fast enough. A white Matiz slammed into the rear of his vehicle, propelling it forward, crashing into Salim and throwing him into the garage and onto the boxes piled inside. The impact knocked the wind out of him. The Matiz continued to rev its engine, pushing Salim's Nexia farther into the garage and onto his prone body, pinning him between the front bumper and the boxes. He heard the Matiz's engine turn off. He tried to move but couldn't. Over the hood of his car, he saw a large figure enter the garage and close the heavy metal doors behind him. The figure approached the front of the Nexia and looked down at him.

Staring at Peter Ivanov's large frame, Salim did not know whether he should be surprised by the encounter. He knew that he had left Peter alive as he raced out of the farmhouse in Uzun. But Salim had expected the man to give up and simply disappear. He had not expected Peter to track him, to seek out vengeance. Salim realized that he had made a mistake in underestimating the American.

Peter had a serious expression on his chiseled face, his slightly crooked nose making him appear menacing. "We have a lot to discuss, my friend. I hope you're in a talking mood." Peter surveyed the various tools on the garage shelves. He finally picked up a set of pliers. He knelt down next to Salim, who was still prone, with his lower body and arms under the car. "You took something that belongs to me, and I'm going to need it back."

Still winded, Salim took in a deep breath. "You are insane. Don't you know that I'm an NSS officer? Do you have any idea the wrath you will bring down upon yourself?"

"You clearly do not understand my situation. I am being blamed for losing eighty kilos of heroin. The heroin that *you* stole from me. I'm now being hunted for losing it. You are going to return it to me or tell me where it is. Otherwise I'll pull out your teeth, one at a time, until you tell me." Peter shook the pliers in front of Salim's face.

"Don't be so naive. You lost the heroin because of your boss, Kurbon Usmanov. He made you his errand boy because you are the only one who does not know that he is on a short list of criminals who are about to go down hard for their activities. Why? Because people like Kurbon do not understand that they need to take certain steps to protect their people and assets by sharing the wealth. I gave him guarantees that only a fool would pass up. He decided to go it alone with his business and put your life at risk. Why else do you think he sent you instead of his nephew? His greediness will be his—and your—downfall. Blame him for your predicament. Not me."

"That was a great speech, but since you still haven't told me where the heroin is, I'm going to follow through on my end of the deal." Peter grabbed Salim's jaw with one hand, and, using his fingers, forced open his lips. Salim wriggled his head and screamed.

Before Peter was able to put the pliers to use, he and his captive heard some commotion outside the garage doors. They heard car doors opening and shutting, and the sound of many feet shuffling outside. Salim's confidence rose, while Peter's face darkened and his brows furrowed. The NSS officer gave a hoarse laugh. "Those are my friends. Your time is up, American. You were at the wrong place at the wrong time. When they kill you, don't take it personally."

The garage doors flew open, and four men in street clothes pointed pistols at Peter. They were Kurbon Usmanov's men. The four stepped back, their pistols still aimed, as a slim figure approached from the darkness behind them. It was Alisher. His serious expression was unreadable. "Hello, Peter," he said flatly.

Alisher's sudden appearance seemed to have surprised Peter, and he remained kneeling, apparently unsure whether his former cellmate had arrived as friend or enemy. Salim lay frozen, his face expressionless.

"Peter, relax. I didn't come to harm you. I came to help you. You can trust me," Alisher said with a weak smile, motioning for Peter to stand up and approach. Peter slowly got up, threw the pliers down on the ground, and walked to Alisher. They shook hands. "Peter, can you wait outside? I'll take care of things here."

Giving one last look at the man pinned to the ground, Peter slowly walked out of the garage. Outside, the night was quiet except for the sound of crickets. The headlights of three black Nexias were flooding the alley with light. These vehicles formed a half circle around the garage, the white Matiz with the shattered front sitting in the center. Alisher took a pistol from one of his men and walked into the dark garage, closing the gray metal doors behind him. His four men walked toward Peter and stood casually around him.

Peter assessed his situation. He told himself that he had a reason to be positive. He, Alisher, Kurbon, and the four men around him were pursuing the same goal, which was to retrieve the narcotics and determine why everything began unraveling, starting in Uzun. What the NSS officer had said in the garage was disturbing, but Peter didn't really care at this point. Maybe they would now find the narcotics, maybe not. Either way, he hoped his name was cleared of stealing the heroin. He no longer cared about the sixty grand that he had hoped to earn. It was too late for that now. Peter just wanted to get the hell out of Uzbekistan. He was operating on the wrong side of the law. He had been found and shot at by New York gangsters, and there was no longer any prospect of making a large sum of money. His only wish now was to tie up all the loose ends and leave the country in one piece, maybe taking Madina along with him.

A single gunshot rang out from the garage. A few seconds later, Alisher walked out through the garage doors. He got into the driver's seat of one of the cars and motioned for Peter to get in. The other four men got into the two remaining Nexias, and the three vehicles pulled out of the alley and drove out of the neighborhood as a convoy.

They began to wind through the darkened streets, the majority of which did not have streetlights. After a moment of silence, Peter asked, "How did you find me?"

Alisher didn't hesitate in responding. "I had you watched. I'll be honest with you; I had ulterior motives for offering you the hotel room last night. Sure, I wanted you to get some rest, but it allowed one of my men to track you from the moment you left the hotel this morning. Otherwise, after leaving you at the cemetery last night, I would have had no way of knowing what you were up to today. Once it became clear that you had found and were tracking the NSS officer involved in stealing the heroin, my man called me."

Another minute of silence passed. The three black Nexias came to a high-speed road and headed toward central Tashkent. Peter asked, "Where are we headed?"

"To the Café Three Oranges. Kurbon wants to speak with you."

"Are you sure that's all he wants to do?"

Alisher smiled. "Yes, of course. We know that what happened in Uzun was out of your control. In fact, you have handled things well. You even led us to the culprit." Peter didn't respond, unconvinced. Alisher continued speaking. "There's something I want to tell you. Mr. Usmanov knows about the debt you owe to a certain Yury Popov in New York. He knows that you are here because you're on the run. I suspect that he offered sixty thousand for trafficking the heroin specifically because that is more or less the amount you need to cover your gambling debt. He knew that you wouldn't pass up on the offer and would accept the job."

"How did he find out about it?"

"A woman tracked you to Tashkent and asked Mr. Usmanov for assistance."

"So, it's not just coincidence that we all came together after our release from Tavaksay Prison," Peter said out loud, though his comment was directed at himself. At that point, he realized that his friendship with Alisher wasn't real. It was only a ploy to get him to work for the Usmanovs. Kurbon, Alisher, and Peter had all seen in each other an opportunity to get something. Alisher needed a promotion, Kurbon needed a trafficker, and Peter needed the money. Anna's reasons were obvious. He came to terms with the fact that he was truly alone in this world. No one could be trusted. Like nomads, they were all traveling through life on their own paths, pursuing their own interests. The only person he could ever count on was himself.

Chapter Nineteen

Ravshan and Kurbon Usmanov were eating dinner at the Café Three Oranges at a corner table. They sat alone while some of their men lingered by the bar. The restaurant had not yet opened for dinner, so they decided to share a meal together. They had spent very little time alone since Alisher and Peter were released from prison. They ate without speaking, however, because their minds were preoccupied with other matters.

Finally, the younger Usmanov spoke. "Uncle, there's something that's been troubling me that I need to speak with you about."

Kurbon looked up from his food, raised his white eyebrows, and nodded to his nephew to continue.

Ravshan set his fork down and asked, "Do you know where Alisher was the entire day Peter left for Uzun?"

Kurbon looked a little surprised by the question. He thought for a moment while swallowing his food. "I recall Alisher telling us that he was going to visit some family. Some family out of town. I can't blame him. After all, he had just been released from prison after being incarcerated for nearly two years."

"Yes, I know. He said he was visiting his parents in Samarqand. The thing is, I called him on his cell phone that day, but a recording said that he was out of the network's calling area. That's fine, given that he was four hours outside of Tashkent, but I tried his parents' home that evening. They told me that they weren't expecting Alisher that day and had only briefly spoken with him since he was released." Ravshan stopped to observe his uncle's reaction.

Kurbon's face was incredulous. "Maybe he was surprising them. Ravshan, I know that you have always been a little envious of Alisher. You haven't liked him since the moment you laid eyes on him. I think maybe you're thinking a little too much about his whereabouts that day. Give him a break."

Ravshan was annoyed by his uncle's dismissal of his observation and his defense of Alisher. He pressed on. "Uncle, how many people knew the exact time, date, and location the heroin was going to be transferred to Peter? Only you, me, Peter, Alisher, and the three dead traffickers. I really doubt that poor family told the NSS where to come and kill them. Plus, they were Tajik. They hate the NSS and Uzbeks in general. Peter had nothing to gain by sabotaging his chances of making a significant amount of money. I'm pretty sure that neither you nor I told the NSS. That only leaves Alisher."

The older Usmanov furrowed his brows while cutting his food, and Ravshan could tell that Kurbon's trust in Alisher wavered momentarily. "I hear what you're saying, but Alisher has no love for the NSS. They are the ones who locked him up."

Ravshan clenched his teeth in frustration. "I know, I know. Something is just not right about him, that's all."

They continued to eat in silence until Kurbon's cell phone rang. He took the call. "Yes. Okay, good. Bring him here." He ended the call and put his cell phone away. He smiled and looked at Ravshan with an "I told you so" look. "That was Alisher. He found Peter and that no-good NSS officer Salim."

Anna drove to Kurbon's bar that evening as scheduled. She parked her car a block away and out of direct line of sight. Once inside, she found him sitting with his nephew at a corner table by the empty dance floor. There were no patrons inside. Only a small handful of his men sat idly around the bar, looking lazy and bored. They paid little attention to her as she approached the table with the two Usmanovs.

"Hello, Anna. Please sit down," Kurbon said as a waiter removed the empty plates of food from the table. "How have you been?"

"Fine," Anna said sitting down across from the two.

"What have you been up to?"

"Not much. Waiting for you to call," Anna said flatly. She couldn't force herself to go through even a minute of small talk.

"Hmm. Well, I'm sorry for the delay. I do have some good news for you. Peter will be here shortly, and you can take him," he said with a smile, looking pleased. Anna thought he was joking. She just looked at him, waiting for him to say as much. She didn't think it would be that easy, and Kurbon could see the incredulity register on her face. "Peter has outlived his usefulness to me. He has finished his errand and returned. I no longer need his services."

"He's not going to want to see me, and he will certainly not leave with me willingly. Can you detain him or keep him somewhere out of the way in order for me to quietly dispose of him?" Anna felt foolish relying on the Usmanovs essentially to do all the work, but she no longer had the resources she needed. She also did not have the expertise to pull together a workable plan immediately on her own. She knew that she was essentially flying by the seat of her pants, hoping to get lucky.

Kurbon appeared annoyed, but after a moment of thought, he said, "I suppose I could occupy him for a bit longer. I can give Peter a small task here in Tashkent and assign my nephew to watch him. Ravshan can keep you abreast of Peter's location, and when you think the time is appropriate, do as you wish."

"That would work well for me." Anna almost thanked him for his graciousness, but wondered if she was playing into his hands. Maybe Kurbon had offered Peter on a silver plate, expecting her to be unprepared for a handover, because he did in fact need Ivanov for another task. Nevertheless, she had to hope for the best. She had no other choice. "If everything goes according to plan, you will have a valuable contact in New York City."

"And if everything goes according to plan, we will not need to see each other again here in Tashkent."

Anna nodded and got up. Kurbon handed her a small piece of paper. "Here's my nephew's number. You two stay in touch."

Anna gave a forced smile and walked out of the bar.

Peter and Alisher arrived at the Café Three Oranges soon after Anna left. Peter was reluctant to enter, not knowing what was in store. He hoped this was the last time he would see the Usmanovs. Inside, he saw the usual faces that he had come to expect. The men greeted Alisher warmly, and he and Peter continued to Kurbon and Ravshan's table, sitting down across from them. Kurbon was smiling, but Peter could tell it was artificial. He certainly had nothing to smile about.

"Peter, it's good to see you again. I'm glad you returned to Tashkent in one piece." Kurbon sounded warm and unnaturally happy, while his nephew sat quietly as usual, looking as if he would rather be somewhere else.

"As you might already know, things didn't go according to plan," Peter said guardedly.

"Yes, I am aware of what happened, my friend. I suspected you of betraying me, but I'm glad that wasn't the case. Alisher defended your honor the entire time. You should really thank him for being your greatest advocate." The last sentence was said with a hint of venom. Neither Alisher nor Peter responded. "So, I hear you two found the culprit."

Alisher leaned forward to speak. "Yes, Kurbonjon, we did. Peter found the NSS officer involved in the attack in Uzun. He tracked him on his own initiative to determine the location of the heroin and called me to assist him. We questioned the officer aggressively, and he admitted to taking the heroin. He did not have it with him, however, nor did he tell us where it was hidden."

"And did you do as I asked?"

"I did. Since he was unwilling to provide any additional information, I killed him." The elder Usmanov nodded in approval. Peter remained silent. Kurbon turned his attention to him.

"Given the circumstances, you did well. I want you to know that. What happened in Uzun was unfortunate, for all of us, but you survived, and you made it back. I haven't forgotten the reason you took this assignment in the first place, Peter. You needed some money before you returned to the United States. I am sympathetic to your needs, and I still want to help you, especially given the hard work you have done for my organization."

Peter wondered what Kurbon was getting at. He had a feeling his business with the Usmanovs was not over. "Thank you, but I don't think I could be of any further service in regard to the lost heroin. Your men seem very capable of handling things from here."

"Yes, my men are very capable. However, you have the guts

and the initiative to follow things through, and you made a lot of progress on your own without any help. So, if I give you some men and some time, I have full confidence you'll find the heroin for me. I need it back, Peter. I can't just forget about eighty kilos. It is worth a very large amount of money, even by American standards." Kurbon reached inside his padded purple robe and pulled out a thin roll of U.S. hundred-dollar bills. He slid it across the table to Peter. "There's five thousand just for your efforts to date. Find the heroin, and I'll triple it."

Peter looked at the money. Money he needed to start over. His goals and dreams hadn't changed, but he was tired of being a criminal. It was not what he wanted, but he had already crossed over to the dark side, so what difference would a little more work make? He would do this one last job, and then that would be it. Then he would leave Uzbekistan. Peter put his hand over the money, and Kurbon smiled. Alisher looked at him but said nothing.

"You made the right choice. You have a bright future. Finish this, and I will leave you in peace. I promise." The elder Usmanov's smile disappeared, and he looked around the table at everyone's faces before coming back to Peter. "Ravshan is going to work with you starting tomorrow. I want you two to start snooping around. Check with our usual sources, shake some guys down, whatever. Let's see who knows what."

Alisher leaned forward, surprised. "But Kurbonjon, I have been involved in this since the beginning. I have already been looking into where the heroin could be. Wouldn't it be better for me to work with Peter on this? No disrespect to you, Ravshanakka."

"No, Alisher, I have other work for you. More important work. I want Ravshan to handle this." His nephew was smirking, no doubt enjoying Alisher's frustration. Alisher leaned back, saying nothing more, but he was clearly confused about Kurbon's reasoning.

Kurbon turned back to Peter. "Ravshan will call you in the morning. Continue to stay at the Grand Orzu hotel until your task is finished. You seem to like it there." He smiled mischievously.

That seemed to be his cue to leave. Peter thanked the Usmanovs and got up, leaving Alisher at the table. By the entrance, he reached past the young male bartender and took a bottle of vodka off the bar shelf. The Uzbek didn't object, probably because of the look Peter gave him. He walked out of the establishment without looking back. Walking into the spring night felt like emerging out of a deep pool of water for air. The tension in the café had been stifling. He walked west the short distance toward his hotel, coughing heavily along the way, blood again covering his hands. He felt eyes on him as he walked through the darkened streets, but he dismissed it, attributing it to paranoia and fatigue.

In the shabby hotel room he had by now gotten used to, he grabbed a small glass off the table and filled it with vodka. He downed the contents in three seconds and filled the glass again. He realized that it had only been four days since he was released from an Uzbek prison. He shook his head in disbelief. If only he had known how events would play out.

Out of the corner of his eye, he saw a shadow under his door linger, moving away a moment later. That was odd, he thought. He was unarmed, so to be safe, he positioned a short but heavy dresser against the door. To stay sharp, Peter thought it best to moderate his drinking, but he still finished half the bottle. Tired and a little inebriated, he fell asleep in no time. During the night, he thought he heard his doorknob turning, but he couldn't be sure.

In the morning, Peter awoke to his cell phone ringing. It was Kurbon's nephew, and he debated not taking the call. But money was money, and the sooner this job ended the better. So he answered the phone. Ravshan wanted him ready in front of the hotel in thirty minutes. Peter said fine.

Thirty minutes later, Peter was sitting in the passenger seat of a BMW. The junior Usmanov didn't say much, so they drove in silence through Tashkent. Peter was content with not talking. He didn't need any new friends, especially now. About twenty minutes later, they entered one of the many poor quarters in Tashkent that was made up of identical white apartment complexes arranged in a circle, with a grass-and-dirt courtyard in the middle. They parked along the corner of one apartment building to observe the stairwell entrance of a building across the courtyard.

After sitting in the parked car in silence for a minute, Ravshan explained what they were doing. "We're waiting for one of our contacts to come out. He's a former militia officer. This guy enriched himself by allowing drug dealers to operate in his jurisdiction. Before he knew it, he was an addict himself and was then fired from the Ministry of Internal Affairs. Now he lives off his relatives. He used to be one of Alisher's regular contacts, but after he went to prison, I started meeting with this junkie."

"Interesting," was all Peter said, even though he didn't really think so. These kinds of contacts were a dime a dozen. You could never really trust what they said, because they would say and do anything for drugs. He decided not to share his opinion with the junior Usmanov. The guy could figure it out for himself.

It was late morning, so most of the foot traffic had passed, and only a few mothers and babushkas were lingering around the unkempt courtyard, chatting among themselves while watching their playing children. Peter and Ravshan observed their behavior in silence until the younger Usmanov again spoke. "So, why did you come to Uzbekistan? Americans don't usually come to this part of the world."

Peter didn't really want to get into this conversation, especially since the Usmanovs already knew the answer, if Alisher was telling the truth. "I just needed a vacation. A long one."

"It's ironic, don't you think? So many Uzbeks would give anything to escape to the United States, but you decided to come here to get away," Ravshan softly chuckled in the driver's seat.

"Yeah, it's ironic."

They sat in silence for a bit longer until Ravshan sat up from his slouched position as a figure emerged from the stairwell they were watching. It was a very thin man, wearing wrinkled clothes that appeared to be two sizes too big for him. He looked tired and walked a bit awkwardly toward an outside bench. He lit a cigarette and sat down. "Let's show him we are here," said the Usmanov as he opened his door and stepped out. Peter did the same. Together, they stood idly next to their car, staring at the man. A moment later, the gaunt man saw them and sat upright in surprise. He glanced around toward the buildings and the stairwell from which he had come. He hesitated a bit, but then got up and walked carefully over to the BMW. As he approached, Peter noticed that he had sunken eyes and pasty skin, as if he had gotten little sun or sleep.

"Ah, hello. I wasn't expecting you. How are you, Ravshanakka? How is your uncle?" the man asked nervously, glancing often at Peter.

"We are all fine, thank you, Sarvar." Ravshan opened a rear door of his car and motioned for the man to enter. He then gestured toward Peter and said to the contact, "Don't worry about him. He's a friend of ours." The addict reluctantly got into the back seat, and Peter and Ravshan got into their seats as well.

Once inside, the two in front turned around to face Sarvar, whose odor was now nauseating. Ravshan led the conversation. "Do you know why we are here?"

"Uh, no."

"We are looking for some narcotics."

"I'm all out. I'm actually looking for some myself."

"In that case, let me help you, and hopefully it will loosen your tongue and make you a bit more cooperative." Ravshan pulled out a small cellophane bag and handed it to the junkie, who snatched it and sniffed it with pleasure.

"You aren't looking for about eighty kilos of heroin are you?" the emaciated man asked wryly.

"And what if I was?" Ravshan asked in surprise.

"I'm just asking because I heard Mr. Usmanov lost a similar amount in transit."

"Is that so?"

"Who knows? I hear things. Maybe it's not true."

"Where would those eighty kilos be right now?"

"I don't really know," Sarvar said nervously, looking out the window.

"Sure you do."

"I really don't."

"That's too bad. I was going to reward you with a kilo if the information turned out to be true." The addict's eyes widened, and it was obvious that he was attempting to do the math on how many months a kilo would last him.

"Well, I did hear a few rumors, but I could really get into a lot of trouble. Will you protect me?"

"Of course."

Sarvar did not seem convinced, but a kilo was a lot of heroin. "I heard a rumor that some government man was sitting on it. He was looking for a buyer, or at least someone to move it out of Tashkent. Sell it somewhere, to someone. He was keeping it in his house, somewhere in the Sabir Rahimov district of Tashkent." Ravshan kept looking intently at the man in the backseat. "That's really all I have. I swear."

Peter wondered if this "government man" was the third gunman in the attack. He was still out there somewhere. It would make sense that he would have it. "That's not enough information. He could be anywhere in that district," the younger Usmanov said with a bit of frustration. The addict just shrugged.

After the meeting, Peter and Ravshan continued to scour the city for information by speaking to every contact Ravshan had on the books. Together, they visited shopkeepers, bazaar vendors, laborers, students, café managers, and waitresses—and of course, militia officers who needed an extra bit of cash. Most didn't know, and many lied purely to make some money. By late afternoon, they still had no good information. The best they had was from their first contact, Sarvar, who knew about the quantity before it was mentioned and confirmed their belief that a security official was safeguarding it.

Ravshan and Peter went to a Uighur restaurant north of Chorsu bazaar for dinner. The Uighurs were an ethnic minority in China, primarily residing in the western Xinjiang region. They were Muslim and Turkic in ethnicity, similar to Uzbeks. A small minority had immigrated to Tashkent over the years. The restaurant had old Turkic paintings on the walls and nondescript furniture with clear plastic table covers. The place was a low-end establishment but was popular for its spicier varieties of Uzbek food. They regrouped at the restaurant with a few of Kurbon's men who had also spent the afternoon looking for leads. They discussed their day over chicken, beef, and lamb *shashlik.* Peter ate *lagman*, a spicy noodle soup with beef and vegetables. Almost everyone's day had been unsuccessful, but one of the men gave a surprising lead of his own. He was large and bald and sweated profusely.

"Some fellow told me that a man living in Sabir Rahimov was holding the heroin. He actually went to see the goods as a prospective buyer but decided not to purchase it because of the high cost."

Ravshan was immediately interested. "Really? Our best lead also points to a man living in the Sabir Rahimov district. Did he give you the address?"

The fat man grinned with his mouth full of food. "Yes, he did."

Ravshan was excited and thought this was his opportunity to prove his leadership to his uncle. He called in the news to the elder Usmanov, who gave the green light to move forward. He sent two men to the address to watch the residence. "Who knows," he said to Peter. "If this gets wrapped up soon, we can go out and celebrate afterward." He was certainly dressed for that possibility.

"Should we call Alisher and give him the news?"

Ravshan's face turned hard. "Alisher can find his own leads. He's got his own agenda, and it's not in line with my family's interests. Plus, he's probably too busy fraternizing with his men to actually do any work."

Peter said nothing, wondering what the source of the animosity was. He was confused about why Ravshan thought Alisher had a different agenda, since all the evidence pointed to his friend doing everything the Usmanovs had asked. Either way, it was none of his business, and he didn't want to get in the middle of their quarrel.

Once all the preparations had been made, the BMW and a black Nexia with five men drove to Sabir Rahimov after dark. When they arrived in the neighborhood, they parked their vehicles down the street from the residence, and Ravshan opened his trunk to reveal a large duffle bag. Opening it, he displayed a small collection of Makarov pistols and AK-47s. "Grab one," he whispered to the men.

They each grabbed a weapon and checked the magazines for ammunition. Peter looked through the bag last, and found only a single drab olive RGD-5 grenade, which was a cheap but effective explosive, common throughout the former Soviet countries. Nothing else. *Great,* he thought. He stuck the grenade in his coat pocket anyway. "Be careful with that," one of the men whispered to him jokingly.

They walked the remaining short distance in silence. As they approached the suspected residence, two men came out of the shadows and approached the group. "Only one person has entered the house, and no one has come out," one of them said quietly. "Otherwise it has been quiet inside."

Ravshan nodded. He told the two to remain outside and keep an eye out. The rest walked to the house doors. As did many middle- to upper-class residential neighborhoods in Tashkent, this street had a continuous, ten-foot high wall running down both sides of the street. Interspersed along the walls were doors and windows that opened into the enclosed front yards of homes. Many of these homes also had large double doors for vehicles to pull into an open air carport, which was essentially a cemented portion of the front yard for parking a car.

At the doors, he gestured for one man to shinny up a drainage pipe and climb over the outside wall. The man tucked his pistol behind him and did as he was told, disappearing over the other side. They heard some rustling behind the door, and a few seconds later, the locks turned and the front door to the yard opened. All of the men poured in quietly. Expecting a confrontation, adrenaline began pumping through Peter's body. He expected that everyone else was also on edge.

They found the yard to be empty. The house was large and curved to the left with the yard. The place looked occupied, and light shined through many of the windows. There was no discernable movement inside, however. Together, the men waited to see if their sounds had alerted anyone. The night was quiet with a crisp, spring evening air. Everything was going well so far, but Peter had a strange feeling in the pit of his stomach.

Ravshan ordered one man to stay by the main entrance to the yard to observe the top floor windows. Two others were asked to stay by the front doors of the house while Ravshan, Peter, and the remaining two men crouched below the windows in the bushes. They slowly moved along the wall toward the left side of the house to peer into the other windows. As they were approaching a window toward the end of the house, they heard muffled chatter ahead of them. Quietly, they approached the window of the room that appeared to be occupied. Together they slowly peered inside, with Ravshan and Peter in the lead. What they discovered froze them in their tracks.

Chapter Twenty

Through the window they saw Salim Guliyamov, the NSS officer with the dark birthmark on his temple, the same man Peter thought Alisher had killed in the garage the previous night. And next to him sat Alisher. In front of them, on a large dining table, were the eighty kilograms of heroin that were stolen in Uzun, stacked in neat square parcels. The two men were speaking to each other over some equipment that rested on the table alongside the heroin. Peter shook his head in wonder. He had been lied to, manipulated, and used by the only person he had trusted. He couldn't wait to leave Uzbekistan.

Ravshan's face was white. "Traitor," he whispered between clenched teeth. He turned around to face his men, but instead faced the muzzle of a pistol pointed at his face. To Peter's and Ravshan's surprise, the two men who were behind them had their pistols drawn and pointed at their heads. From around the corner, the three men posted at the front doors and yard also approached, pistols drawn. Peter and Ravshan stood frozen, outnumbered and outgunned, wondering what was happening. It all felt like a bad dream. One of the men tapped the window, and Alisher and Salim, who immediately stopped speaking, motioned for everyone to come inside as if they were signaling for their children to come in for dinner, not at all taken aback at discovering the group of men outside.

The five men, who now appeared to be following Alisher's orders, nudged their two captives toward the front entrance. Peter was genuinely surprised. He was also relieved, however, that this entire situation had finally come to an end. There were no more questions. There was no more chasing. No more endless tasks that kept him bound to the Usmanovs.

The two captives were escorted through the front doors, where they were met by Salim and Alisher, who were standing in the foyer. Alisher was looking sharp, wearing a black suit with a dark gray button-down shirt. Salim looked haggard and tired by comparison. The NSS officer carefully took Ravshan's weapon and handcuffed him and Peter, giving the latter a dirty look. The other men lowered their weapons and relaxed.

Alisher had a serious expression on his face with a hint of sadness as he looked at his old cellmate. "I'm sorry for making you a part of this. This wasn't the way I expected this to happen." His gaze shifted to Ravshan, and his face took on a cruel expression. "However, the fact that events led to a meeting like this was unavoidable. It became unavoidable the day Kurbon Usmanov decided that enriching himself was more important than taking care of his people. The day his ego trumped rationality."

Alisher spread his arms toward the five men standing guard behind the prisoners. "Mr. Usmanov always spoke about his 'organization.' But *we* are the organization, not him alone. He never understood that." He pointed a finger at a frightened Ravshan. "But you are far worse. You betrayed me. While I was in Tavaksay prison, Salim here approached me and told me about the first time you and he had met. How could you, Ravshan? What did I ever do to you?"

Ravshan's chin quivered with shame and fear. Alisher continued, "Even after I was arrested, Salim offered your uncle a way to save me, but Kurbon instead decided to save his money by bargaining on the amount he was willing to pay for my release. Neither of you thought I would discover the real reason why I rotted in jail for almost two years." He lowered his voice. "You and your uncle never even tried to protect me from the dozens of merchants and smugglers who were sent to the same prison as me. I had no choice but to look after myself. Only the NSS assured my safety." Alisher's voice dropped to a whisper. "Well, it didn't take much convincing. I was happy to do it after being betrayed by you and Mr. Usmanov."

Ravshan had tears streaming down his face, but he mustered some courage and raised his chin. "We enriched you! We gave you everything you have. If it wasn't for us, you would still be selling fake carpets alone at the bazaars, struggling to get by. We saw potential in you and gave you an opportunity. After all that, you treat me this way. Like a prisoner." Ravshan saw Alisher's face harden. "I am an Usmanov!" he pleaded in desperation.

Alisher quickly drew a pistol from a shoulder holster hidden under his suit jacket and, pointing it at Ravshan's head, fired. The shot startled Peter and the men around them. The echo vibrated through the house. The younger Usmanov's body crumpled to the floor. "You were," Alisher muttered.

Peter expected to be executed next. For a moment, everyone stood silently and watched the bleeding body. Then Alisher reholstered his weapon. "I'm not going to kill you, Peter. You're not a part of this." Taking the keys from Salim, he unlocked Peter's handcuffs and took them off. "Don't worry, Peter. You will get to leave this country safely."

The men standing around them picked up Ravshan's body and carried it outside, leaving a large pool of blood on the tile floor. Salim gave Peter a long, hard look and walked back to the dining room, leaving him alone with Alisher in the foyer.

Peter remained motionless, still in shock. "I feel like a pawn in a big game."

Alisher smirked. "Unfortunately, you were. You're not going to like hearing this, but I was the third gunman down in Uzun. The fact that you survived the attack and returned to Tashkent in one piece was not just luck. Salim wanted to give your description to the border guards. I had to convince him not to. I faced a lot of resistance to that, especially after you killed an officer. But you were never in any real danger. I did have to make sure you didn't ruin our plans. If I hadn't had you watched, you might have killed

Salim, which would have been very unfortunate, since he was going to ensure that my men and I could operate in the narcotics business without any future trouble."

"Well, I'm glad I was of assistance," Peter sighed, letting the tension slip out of his body. *What a night,* he thought.

"I need you to return to your hotel room. I will meet you there in the morning. Kurbon is expecting to hear back from his nephew this evening. My men and I still have some work to do."

"I need to get out of here. Out of Tashkent. I don't want anything more to do with any of this."

"I understand, but you need to be patient and stay hidden. It's in your best interest. If Kurbon sees you out and about, your life could be in danger. When this is all over, I will find you. Trust me."

Peter nodded and left the house, out to the darkened street. He saw two of the Usmanovs' men standing in the shadows, but they just let him walk by.

Back in his hotel room, Peter finished the vodka that was left in the bottle he had taken out of the Café Three Oranges. He was still jittery from the evening's events. He turned on the television to some Russian language channel, but he was too distracted by his thoughts to pay attention to what was on. He decided to call Madina. If he was to leave Uzbekistan quickly, he wanted to see her one last time. He wished he didn't have to leave her. Seeing her was exhilarating, and he had never felt this way about a woman before. He knew his strong feelings were unnatural, since they had spent very little time together, but he had few bright spots in his life. It was around midnight, but he dialed her number anyway, hoping she would answer.

"Peter?" she asked as if she was unsure.

"Hello, Madina." His voice sounded heavy. "Yes, it's me."

"How are things?"

"Things are fine, but I need to leave Uzbekistan soon. I wish I could stay longer, but I can't. I was hoping we could see each other tomorrow morning. I want to see you one last time."

"You are leaving? Why so suddenly?" she asked, disappointment in her voice.

"Business reasons. I'm sorry. I wish we had more time together. I really wanted to spend more time with you," Peter said, nervous about being so frank about his emotions, but hating to end something that had begun so well.

"Peter, I like you. I'm a little upset that you are leaving so soon."

It pained him to hear that. "I don't really know where I'm going to be, but maybe you can join me soon. At least for a little while, if it's possible. I can show you what things are like outside of Uzbekistan." His tone turned serious, and he felt foolish about what he was about to say. "I want to see you again Madina, and I'm not just talking about tomorrow."

"Visit you? Are you serious?" she asked slowly, clearly nervous but also excited. "I have to see, but I'm sure I could."

"Let's talk about it tomorrow. I want to discuss this in person. Can I see you?"

"Yes, of course. When? Where?"

"Meet me at Amir Timur Square at the center of town. How about eleven in the morning?"

"Um, okay. I will see you then."

"Good. I can't wait."

"Me neither. Bye."

He had not planned on telling her that he wanted her to come along. It had just slipped out, but he realized that he meant it. Still fully clothed, he lay in his bed and reflected back on everything that had happened over the past five days. He was still no better off than he had been when he arrived in the country, with only a little money to his name. He wondered what he would do now. He wondered where he could go and start over. He really needed to do something less stressful. More peaceful, and with Madina. With these thoughts of the future, he drifted off.

Kurbon Usmanov stayed late at the Café Three Oranges to go over the accounting books. He realized with distress that he had very little money left. He thought he could still survive this little crisis, however, especially if his nephew returned with the missing heroin. He would prosper, he reassured himself.

He heard the door open. The place was empty except for three men sitting idly by the bar to escort him home. To his mild surprise, Alisher walked in—oddly, with six of Kurbon's own men. They were quiet and said nothing. Alisher walked alone, slowly, to Kurbon's table with a gloomy, serious expression on his face.

"May I sit?" Alisher asked once he reached the table.

"Sure," Kurbon said guardedly. He was tired, and it showed on his face. He wondered what this visit was about. "It's late. What do you need, Alisher?"

"Actually, nothing." Alisher spoke slowly in an even voice. He was leaning forward in his chair, with his arms under the table. "I have some news for you, Mr. Usmanov. Ravshan was not able to retrieve the heroin. He's dead."

Kurbon looked into Alisher's eyes and knew that he spoke the truth. "How could that have happened?" He choked back tears.

"You killed him, Mr. Usmanov. Your decisions led to his death."

Usmanov's sadness turned to anger as he looked at Alisher, and his words sank in. "What did you say to me? How dare you speak to me that way?!" He looked toward the men standing nervously by the bar, but they turned away from his gaze, doing nothing. It dawned on Kurbon that his men had turned on him. They had mutinied.

Alisher let the significance of the moment settle in. Kurbon realized that his life was coming to an abrupt end. This was not how he had envisioned things. Not this way. He noticed that Alisher, the man he trusted and loved like a son, had tears in his eyes.

In a soft voice, Alisher finally said, "You have done a lot for me, Mr. Usmanov. I appreciate how you took me in. I'm sorry it has to end this way."

Kurbon swallowed some tears and lifted his chin up, straightening his clothes to appear more regal. He knew what was coming. "I'm sorry, too." He smiled weakly.

A shot rang out, and Kurbon felt his guts explode, blood splattering up onto his face. Alisher's arms were still hidden, but a wisp of smoke rose from under the table. As Kurbon slowly died, the last thing he saw was his men lowering their heads and turning away.

Peter woke up in the early morning, completely dressed, with his boots and leather jacket still on. The sky was a dark gray, the sun beginning to rise in the distance. His exhaustion must have knocked him out. He slowly got up and walked to the bathroom, where he splashed some water on his face. He looked closely at his reflection. He thought he appeared slimmer and older than when he first arrived in the country. A vacation would fatten him up and make him feel younger, he thought. The television was still on, the volume low. There was some breaking news. A prominent businessman with ties to the criminal underworld had been shot at a local bar. Details were still pending.

There was a knock at the door. Nervous, Peter walked to it and listened. "Peter, it's me." It was the only voice he expected. He opened the door and let his friend in. Alisher was wearing the same suit as the night before. He walked in and took off his suit jacket, throwing it on the bed. He looked more tired than Peter. He had a thick manila envelope in his hand.

"There was some breaking news on television," Peter said offhandedly.

Alisher smiled weakly. "Yes, I suppose there would have been. There will no doubt be an investigation, but it will end quietly and inconclusively."

Peter nodded.

"You need to leave the country. Salim insists. So, this will most likely be the last time we see each other." Alisher handed Peter the manila envelope. "This is for you."

Peter opened it and stared at a thick stack of crisp U.S. bills. "That's twenty thousand dollars," Alisher said, smiling.

Peter alternated skeptical glances between his former cellmate and the contents of the envelope. "I don't really know what to say," he said, smiling. It was a pleasant, unexpected surprise.

"It's no problem. It's the most I could spare." Then, after an awkward moment, "You're a good friend, Peter. You're the only real friend I have. I owe you my life."

"It's nothing." Then, not knowing what else to say, he said, "Best of luck to you in your future endeavors. I have a feeling you will be very successful."

"I hope you're right," Alisher said, smiling broadly. He then turned and walked out of the hotel room. "Good-bye, Ivanov. Stay in touch," he said before closing the door behind him.

Alone again in his hotel room, Peter immediately flipped

through the envelope one more time, expecting the money to have disappeared as if Alisher had played a big joke. It was still there. Twenty thousand dollars meant a new life somewhere. He wanted to celebrate. It pained him to leave Uzbekistan, regardless of what he had been through. It just didn't feel like the right time to leave.

He then noticed Alisher's suit jacket lying on the bed. He grabbed it and opened the door to catch up to his friend.

Anna fired three rounds into Peter's chest, throwing him back into the room. She had fired without thinking. She did it more out of surprise at having the door unexpectedly open than as a planned attack. She had been walking past his room to a waiting spot down the hallway. Before she knew it, she had done what she came to do. She gathered her nerves and cautiously stepped into the room, not knowing what to expect.

Peter was lying on his stomach, squirming on the floor, gurgling blood onto the linoleum. There were three holes in the back of his black leather jacket, the bullets having gone cleanly through. At that moment, Anna felt remorse for what she had done. She had killed a man. She had been waiting for this moment for a very long time, but now that it had arrived, she felt a pang of sadness. Well, she had done her job. Her father would be proud.

Peter slowly rolled over, his hands balled against his chest. His white shirt was crimson, and blood was trickling out of his mouth. He looked at Anna and held her eyes. Shock and pain painted his pale face. His feet weakly kicked the ground a few times, lacking the strength to push his body. He struggled to speak at first, but he finally hissed, "You win. It must feel good."

Anna was standing above Peter with her pistol still pointed at him. Sunlight shone through the window onto Peter's body as if a spotlight was directed at him. Even though she had Peter where she wanted him, she was frightened. She had never shot anyone before. She stared at his form, not knowing what to do next. But something wasn't right. She looked closely at his hands and realized that one hand was gripping something. It was a grenade. Peter's hand was squeezing the grenade's lever against its body, keeping the fuse from igniting. He was mortally wounded, however, and his grip was weakening. If he didn't release the lever intentionally, he would after he died. It dawned on Anna that, either way, she would be killed seconds later. Knowing that she had no escape, she lost her strength to stand. She slowly moved to the bedside and sat down. "Actually, it doesn't," she choked.

Peter looked curiously at Anna. He winced in pain and lightly felt his chest wounds, which were hemorrhaging blood all over his shirt. "I—I wish you hadn't come," he said quietly, his breath slowing. "Things were turning around for me."

Anna's eyes were glazed and she sat very still. From her seated position she could look out the window, onto Shota Rustavelli, where she could see the early morning traffic. It all seemed so far away. "I wish I hadn't come either. This isn't me." She gave a weak smile and looked again at Peter. "I'm sorry."

His eyes struggled to stay open. The pool of blood under his body continued to expand. "It doesn't matter," he whispered, his eyes closing. "This is my fate. Good things don't happen to me."

Peter's hands fell to his sides, and his grip on the grenade loosened, causing it to roll past his fingertips towards Anna. Anna noticed but continued to stare out the window.

The explosion that tore through the hotel could be heard for miles. Pedestrians on nearby streets saw a blast of flame and debris fly out the hotel windows, followed by a thick plume of smoke that billowed out toward the blue sky. Children walking to school huddled closer to their parents. Cars driving by pulled over and stopped, and people came out to the street to see what had happened. Bricks and glass were scattered everywhere, but the street was otherwise eerily silent.

Madina arrived a little early to Amir Timur Square. She was excited about the previous night's conversation with Peter but also a little anxious about what he had to say. She had only met him a few days ago, she told herself. It was too soon to speak so seriously, but it felt natural.

The weather was beautiful, and there were many early morning pedestrians cutting through the square. She sat on a metal bench in the shade with thin rays of sun streaking through the tree foliage above her. She looked expectedly at everyone who walked by, but none of them were Peter. At eleven thirty, she became a little annoyed. She called his cell phone and got no answer. She tried again at twelve, but she still couldn't reach him.

She continued to wait. If he needed to leave the country soon, she wanted to see him one last time. It was worth the wait.

She began walking around the green areas of the square, wondering if he was waiting in some hidden corner, but he was nowhere in sight. She sat on the bench at the foot of Tamerlane's statue. She waited until 1:00 PM. She hoped that Peter was okay. She wondered if he had gotten cold feet, regretting what he had said the previous night. She called one last time and then walked away, toward the tram station. She needed to get ready for work and couldn't wait forever. She was upset but still hoped that he would call.

Epilogue

In May 2005, an uprising took place in Andijon, a small town in a poor and increasingly discontented region of Uzbekistan known as the Fergana Valley. Armed Uzbek men raided and took over the town's main administrative building, killed a number of officials, and freed all the convicts imprisoned inside. They then rallied hundreds of local residents into the town's adjoining square to use as a human shield against the expected response by Uzbekistani security forces. The crowd also protested gas shortages and other economic hardships, which the insurgents captured on video to broadcast to the world. The Uzbekistani government believed the region's stability was threatened and feared that a ripple effect would reach the capital of Tashkent. Security forces responded to the threat in Andijon and armed conflict ensued. The insurgency was successfully put down, but many innocent bystanders died in the crossfire.

Western countries condemned the government's harsh response to what they believed was a peaceful protest, and the United States asked for an independent investigation into the events. Uzbekistan's President Karimov felt betrayed by the United States, and suspected U.S.–funded democratization NGOs of being responsible for the demonstrations that took place. Pro-democracy revolutions had overthrown governments in Georgia, Ukraine, and Kyrgyzstan during this same period. The United States denied these allegations and did not relent in its condemnation over the following months. As a result, Uzbekistan's relationship with the United States slowly deteriorated.

President Karimov asked the U.S. military to withdraw completely from Karshi-Khanabad (K2), and in November 2005, American forces left Uzbekistan. The United States and the European Union banned Uzbek leaders who were connected to the Andijon security response from obtaining visas to visit their countries. As of fall 2008, relations between Uzbekistan and the United States were at their lowest point since the country achieved independence in 1991.

Afghanistan continues to be the world's biggest producer of heroin, accounting for over 90 percent of the world's total supply. A large portion of Afghan heroin is trafficked through Central Asian countries like Uzbekistan. High unemployment and low wages compel the poor residents who live along the border regions of Central Asian countries to get involved in trafficking the narcotics. These traffickers often work in coordination with corrupt Central Asian government and law enforcement officials to ensure that the product reaches Russian and European markets.

CPSIA information can be obtained at www.ICGtesting.com
Printed in the USA
LVOW12s2150251113

362837LV00001B/119/P